Rebel against Love

by

ELIZABETH ASHTON

Harlequin Books

TORONTO • LONDON • LOS ANGELES • AMSTERDAM
SYDNEY • HAMBURG • PARIS • STOCKHOLM • ATHENS • TOKYO

Original hardcover edition published in 1981
by Mills & Boon Limited

ISBN 0-373-02444-4

Harlequin edition published December 1981

His kisses sent her into a blind fury

"If you wanted to punish me for being impertinent," Jo snapped, "I'd much rather you'd beaten me!"

"I may be provoked into doing that if you aren't more civil, but I find it more amusing to teach you to become a woman."

"Oh, you...you!" she raged.

Marcel laughed. "You show every sign of being an apt pupil—there is plenty of passion in you."

Jo took a step forward, wanting to hit him, and her foot touched his riding crop. Quick as thought she snatched it and struck him across his mocking face. Then, without waiting to see the damage, she fled toward the horses. She loosed them both and mounted, galloping recklessly down the woodland track as if all the devils in hell were in pursuit.

CHAPTER ONE

EARLY morning sunshine flooded the yard and sent bright shafts through the open door of the stable and an inquisitive hen peered inside hoping to pick up some dropped corn. A girl was grooming a bay thoroughbred mare, whistling while she worked. She might easily have been taken for a boy, for she was dressed in jeans, sweater and wellington boots, with a man's cap covering her head to protect her hair from dust and chaff. The grey gelding, Captain, in the next stall munched contentedly at the feed she had just given him.

The girl broke into song. 'Oh, what a beautiful morning, Oh, what a beautiful day,' she carolled—and stopped abruptly, for her quick ear caught the sound of footsteps crossing the yard. The mare, Bonny, threw up her head and rolled the whites of her eyes, while Captain pricked his ears. The hen rushed away with a cackle, as a man's figure darkened the doorway. The girl turned round, dandy brush in hand to face the intruder.

'Hi, *mon garçon!*'

The French words identified him. He was Marcel de Savigny, who had arrived the previous evening to view the stallion colt Roger Thornton, the girl's father and owner of Greyfriars Farm, hoped to sell to him. As she said nothing, he went on:

'I wish to ride—your boss has given me permission. He said I should find Joe here. You are perhaps this Joe?'

The girl suppressed a giggle, realising that she had been mistaken for a stable boy, which was not surprising, since the sloppy sweater she had put on against the morning chill disguised any feminine curves, and the cap obscured her hair. She had missed his arrival the night before, having gone to a disco session with her current boy-friend, Terry Robinson. Roger had omitted to mention that 'Joe' was one of his daughters. Her name was Josephine, but by her own wish she was always called Jo. Because she could never resist an opportunity for a mischievous prank, Jo touched her cap and said with her best Suffolk drawl:

'That be roight, sir, I be Joe.'

'*Eh bien*, Joe, please to saddle the horse for me.'

'Wot 'orse du ee want to roide, sir, and in't the boss agoin' wi' yu?'

'No, and the animal is naturally the black stallion— Lucifer, I believe you call him.'

His English was very good, if a little stilted. He spoke arrogantly, as if accustomed to giving orders, and his tone instantly put Jo's back up. Nor did she want Lucifer to go to France; she had known the beast since he was foaled and he was more amenable to her handling than any man's, though she was forbidden to ride him. She was surprised her father was allowing this stranger to take the horse out without his supervision, and forgetting her pose, she said doubtfully:

'Luci is a stallion, we don't use him for hacking.'

The Frenchman laughed and made a coarse joke about mares and stallions, which would have been appreciated by a boy, but caused Jo to blush. She hastily turned away, and Marcel de Savigny said sharply:

'Leave your other duties, *mon garçon*, and do as I tell you. I have not all the morning to waste.'

The command annoyed her, and '*garçon*' was how waiters were addressed in France, wasn't it? She moved out of Bonny's stall, putting down her brush, remarking that Lucifer could be 'a little old devil' with strangers.

'So I am told, but I can handle devils,' he retorted confidently.

'Then Oi reckon if the boss say so, it be okay.'

'Of course it is—do you usually query your boss's orders?' Marcel de Savigny snapped.

Jo flushed at the rebuke.

'No, sir, that be more'n my place is worth. If yu'll step aside, sir, Oi'll get 'is tack.'

He moved out of the doorway to allow her to pass him. Jo went into the tackroom adjoining the stable and lifted down a saddle and bridle. Rejoining him in the yard, she was able to see him clearly in full light. He was taller than she was, and she was a tall girl, and had the light, wiry build of the true horseman; she had been told he bred horses as did her father. He was swinging his riding cap in long, nervous fingers, and his bared head was covered with thick dark hair; his features were aquiline, but surprisingly the eyes surveying her quizzically were a vivid blue in his dark face. He wore breeches, polished boots and a yellow sweater, and was impeccably groomed, which only antagonised her the more, for Terry Robinson belonged to the hirsute, leather-jacketed brigade, and despised sartorial elegance, terming it cissy, but there was nothing effeminate about Marcel de Savigny; he emanated virility and leashed force, and instinctively Jo resented his masculine challenge. He was too confident and assured—cocky was the word she used to herself—and she hoped very much that Lucifer would throw him. She humped the saddle on her shoulder, and forgetting he believed her to be a boy, was put out that he did not offer to carry it for her. She crossed the yard to where a wicked black head was thrust out over the half door.

She slipped the bridle over the beast's head, then opened the door and went in to saddle him. Lucifer made no protest, nuzzling her shoulder. He had known her all his life. He was a big horse, sixteen hands, with a broad chest and powerful quarters. He was coal black all over without a white hair upon him. But when Jo led him out into the yard and Marcel de Savigny approached him, his head went up and his ears went back. To Jo's delight he showed every sign of refusing to allow the stranger to mount him, a not uncommon occurrence.

'*Ah, il est magnifique!*' Marcel de Savigny exclaimed, his experienced eye noticing the animal's good points.

He took the reins from Jo, and the horse started back, rolling his eyes. Jo retreated, prepared to enjoy the circus.

Marcel de Savigny was murmuring soft words in his own tongue, while retaining a close hold on the bridle. Lucifer stood still, and he gently stroked the satin neck. The animal quivered, then the flattened ears pricked forward as if to catch a whispered message. Communion had been established between man and horse, and Lucifer was meekly submissive as Marcel de Savigny swung himself into the saddle.

Unwillingly Jo had to concede that he looked remarkably well on a horse; he had an excellent seat, and his hands were light but firm. He held his dark head as proudly as did the stallion he bestrode; they were well matched, both showing breeding in every line of their respective shapes.

Jo recalled that her father had told her the de Savignys were descended from the old French aristocrats. They had been comtes in a less democratic age—not that she considered aristocratic lineage to be an asset. She herself was of good yeoman stock, and Terry had no ancestry to speak of. They had decided that such attributes were outdated and pretentious. Though she appreciated a thoroughbred horse, pride of birth in a human she termed 'side'. Marcel de Savigny, she decided, was a proud, arrogant man, to be avoided as much as possible—but he certainly had a way with horses.

The connection between the Thorntons and de Savignys dated since the war. Roger's elder brother had been shot down over France, and the de Savignys had hidden him on their estate. Her uncle John had not long survived the war, and his hosts had expressed their sorrow to learn of his decease. Roger had met them then and several times since, and they frequently exchanged breeding stock, but Jo had had no contact with them, and the wartime story was before her and Marcel's time. He had succeeded to his father's domain, and was almost a stranger to them.

Marcel walked Lucifer round the yard as if to accustom the horse to his control, and as he passed Jo he dropped a couple of coins at her feet.

'Buy yourself a drink,' he said carelessly.

He urged the stallion to a trot and rode out of the yard into the early summer morning. He had been proved right, he could handle devils, but what magic he had used was incomprehensible to Jo.

'Luci, you're a traitor,' she murmured, for she had been defrauded of the display of temper which she had expected would unseat this arrogant stranger and humiliate him. Instinctively she felt that Marcel was an enemy, a supporter of the establishment, which she spent much of her young life seeking to defy. Not that her parents were strict, the atmosphere at Greyfriars was tolerant and carefree, and since she had turned eighteen they had made no attempt to discipline her; they trusted to her own good sense and their mutual affection to keep her out of mischief. But Marcel de Savigny was of a different calibre. She was sure he was a martinet who would expect all his associates to conform, which was unjust for she knew nothing about the man beyond his autocratic air which had antagonised her. She glanced scornfully at the coins at her feet, wishing she had thrown them at him, then recollecting her masquerade she picked them up. She would return them to Marcel when he had discovered his mistake and she hoped he would be disconcerted.

Jo completed her morning chores, which included turning a couple of brood mares with foals at foot out to graze. Then she went to the milking shed, where Bert the cowman was finishing his morning task, removing the apparatus from the cows' udders. Jo helped him to release the Friesians from their stalls and the patient beasts plodded out of the byre towards their pasture. The Thorntons did not keep many cows, their principal activity being arable crops.

Bert and Jo followed the herd and after securing the gate behind them, turned to survey the hayfield next door. It was a perfect June morning and looked set fair.

'We'll start cutting next week if the weather holds,' Jo suggested, and Bert nodded. The grass was in flower and ready for harvesting. Beyond the hayfield were acres of wheat and barley, green and level, barely tinged with gold.

'If the weather holds,' he said lugubriously, weather being the farmer's continual anxiety.

As Jo went back into the yard, Marcel returned. The black's glossy neck was streaked with foam and she looked at him reproachfully.

'He's very hot.'

'He will take no harm if you rub him down,' Marcel told her, not noticing she had spoken in her normal voice. 'He needed a gallop, didn't you, *mon vieux*?' He slapped the animal's neck. 'Do not let him drink until he has cooled off.'

Jo bit back a retort demanding who he thought he was talking to, as if she did not know that and more as well as he did, but she was not yet ready to reveal herself. As she led Lucifer into his box she was savouring his confusion when later on she was introduced to him as a daughter of the house. Frenchmen were supposed to be gallant, weren't they? He would be put out when he discovered she was a girl.

Marcel strode off towards the house whistling gaily. He acts as though he owns the place, Jo thought dourly. That he was undeniably good-looking, even attractive, only added to her resentment. She rubbed Lucifer down, fed him and went towards the house and breakfast, but whereas Marcel had entered by the front door, she went round to the back.

The farmhouse was roomy and rambling. Downstairs, the three front rooms, office, dining room and sitting room, were connected by a passage behind them. There were two staircases, the main one being opposite the front entrance, a second one going up from the kitchen, concealed by a latched door. The kitchen, scullery, dairy and larder were behind the front rooms separated from them by a bisecting passage. The first, with its red-tiled floor and Aga stove, was a cheerful place and always warm even on the coldest days. A square wooden table stood in the centre of it, covered by a check cloth. Mr and Mrs Thornton ate in the dining room, but Jo seldom bothered to join them for breakfast. She and her younger sister Jess preferred to get what they wanted, when they wanted it, informally in the kitchen. As Jo came in, Jess was sitting at the table consuming a large plateful of bacon and eggs. There were three Thornton sisters, Alison, the eldest, three years older than Jo; Josephine, now nineteen, and Jessica—Jess—a lively sixteen-year-old just left school, who had taken a commercial course and helped her father as his secretary. The Thorntons had hoped for a son, but gave up when the third daughter made her appearance. Alison had been accepted as a girl and developed into a dainty, feminine creature like her mother, but the two younger ones had been brought up as boys, their father encouraging their eager interest in the farm and its running. With mechanisation, women could contribute much to farming. Jo drove the tractor and other machines, and could perform most of the tasks as well as a man except for the heavy lifting. The horses were a sideline, and a bribe; as long as there were riding horses, Jo was content to live and work on the farm. Her ambition was to be a show jumper and from an early age she had competed in local gymkhanas.

'Hi!' Jess said with her mouth full. 'I've cooked your grub, you'll find it in the hot cupboard.'

'Bless you,' Jo returned gratefully, retrieving her plate. 'I'm famished!'

'Seen His Nibs this morning?' Jess went on, putting bread in to the toaster.

'If you mean our French guest, he blew into the

stables this morning and demanded a mount as if I were one of his serfs.'

'But didn't he know who you were?'

'No, we've not been introduced.' Jo's eyes sparkled with mischief. 'He thought I was a groom and I played up to him. He wanted to ride Lucifer.'

'Really?' Jess looked startled. 'Did the colt throw him?'

'Unfortunately no. He seems to have a way with horses.'

'Not only with horses,' Jess informed her. 'Of course, you weren't here for dinner last night . . . where were you, by the way? Out with Terry?'

'What do you think? I decided there were enough of you to entertain him without me. Bet you had a boring evening.'

'Not at all. Mr de Savigny was very amusing, and he's quite a dish, even at his age.'

To Jess anyone over thirty was ancient, and Marcel de Savigny was past his first youth, though still a year short of thirty.

'Ally's fallen for him, hook, line and sinker,' Jess concluded.

'She would,' Jo commented, accepting a piece of toast. 'She can't resist a stuffed shirt if it's well tailored, and judging by his riding outfit, he's one for dress.'

'But he must be something if he can handle Lucifer.'

'Hypnotism,' Jo declared, who was resentful that her father would not allow her to ride the beast herself. 'He whispered in his ear, and *voilà*! as they say in his tongue.'

Jess giggled. 'It isn't only horse's ears he whispers into.'

'That sort, is he?' Jo was disdainful.

'Well, he's French.'

'He didn't waste any charm on me, but of course he thought I was a scruffy boy.'

'I'm not surprised.' Jess ran a critical eye over her sister's apparel. 'You do rather overdo the gamine touch.'

'I leave the feminine frills to Ally. Strange she should be so different from us.'

Jess and Jo were very alike, the same broad foreheads, level dark brows and big grey eyes, but whereas Jess's hair was brown, Jo's was the colour of a ripe horse-chestnut. She was taller than her sister and still moved with the awkward grace of a young colt.

'She takes after Mum,' Jess explained. 'We're like Dad. Also they brought her up to be a lady, select boarding school and all that, but it was rather expensive, so we were allowed to run wild.'

'Thank God for that,' Jo said fervently. 'I'd hate to have to try to be refined.'

'But Ally's not missish,' Jess defended her sister, 'she's only developed her feminine wiles. You should have seen her practising them last night.'

'Was the snob impressed?' Jo asked casually.

'Jo, you mustn't call him that!' Jess threw an apprehensive glance towards the door.

'I'll call him what I please—behind his back,' Jo declared. 'But let's talk of something more interesting. Bert's talking about starting haysel.'

As they finished their meal, Alison came in carrying a tray loaded with utensils from the dining room. Smaller than her sisters, she was very pretty, her hair so dark as to be almost black, with a pink and white complexion which she tended carefully, and a neat rounded figure. Only her grey eyes resembled her sisters.

'Aren't you coming to help clear?' she asked.

'Have a heart, I'm only just in from the stables,' Jo protested.

'And look like it, even to the straw in your hair.'

Jo stood up and wandered over to look in the small mirror hanging above the sink. She had left her cap in the stables, and there was straw in her hair. She produced a pocket comb and drew it through her thick locks.

'Sign of honest toil,' she observed. 'We outdoor girls can't be immaculate like you hothouse plants.'

Alison was wearing well cut brown slacks and a suede waistcoat over a white blouse, which showed the elegant lines of her slim waist and rounded hips. Her hair was smooth as silk.

'You delight in looking a mess,' Alison returned, 'and someone has to do the indoor chores, which I'll admit I prefer to mucking out stables.'

Annette Thornton did the cooking and Alison the housework, with a Mrs Young coming in to do the rough.

Jessica said: 'What's happened to your French beau?'

'If you mean Mr de Savigny, Daddy's taking him into Dunwich in the car. It seems he's read about the city under the sea, though we all know there's nothing left but sand. They'll be back for lunch.'

'Do we have to call him "Mr"?' Jess enquired.

'Certainly—the French are more formal than we are,' Alison told her repressively. 'And Jo, for heaven's sake make yourself look respectable.' She glanced disgustedly at her sister's by no means clean jeans.

'Oh, I shan't come in,' Jo decided. 'I'll take a hunk of bread and cheese and eat it in the stables. I plan to take Bonny over the sticks this afternoon.'

'You prefer hobnobbing with the farmhands to civilised company?' Alison enquired scornfully.

'They're more my sort, and Terry'll be looking in during the lunch hour, which he calls dinner time, to show me his new motorbike.'

'That yob!'

'He isn't a yob, he's a good pal, and you needn't turn up your aristocratic nose at him. His father does own their garage.'

'But it's not as impressive as a château,' Jess suggested, giving her sister a sly glance.

Alison coloured faintly as she said hastily;

'Mr de Savigny is probably engaged to some suitable partner back home, it's the way they do things in France.'

'But that wouldn't stop him from having a bit of fun on the side,' Jo said flippantly.

'Don't be coarse,' Alison flashed back at her. 'I'm sure Mr de Savigny is a gentleman.'

'They're the worst of the lot,' Jo declared. 'Okay, Ally, keep your hair on,' as Alison flushed angrily. 'I was only thinking that if he is affianced—isn't that the way they put it?—we'd better keep our hearts from straying in his direction.'

'Do control that tongue of yours,' Alison snapped.

'I was only trying to warn you, dear sister.'

'Quite unnecessary,' Alison returned. 'Just because I took the trouble to try to make a stranger and a foreigner feel at home, you jump to ridiculous conclusions.' She looked accusingly at Jessica. 'What have you been saying?'

Jess shrugged her shoulders. 'Nothing. I only told Jo he was a dish.'

'Absurd expression,' Alison said scornfully, and stalked out with her head in the air.

The other two girls exchanged glances.

'Definitely smitten,' Jo decided.

'Perhaps there isn't a fiancée in France?' Jess hazarded.

'Good lord, I'd hate to have that snotty male for a brother-in-law,' Jo exclaimed in alarm.

'He won't be staying long enough for anything serious to develop,' Jess told her comfortably. Then Mrs Young came in to start work, and the conversation was closed.

There was a lull in farming operations between the end of the spring sowing and the beginning of haytime, so Jo had plenty of time to devote to her riding. She spent the morning cleaning tack, and ate her alfresco lunch in the barn. She smiled to herself as she thought of her sisters and parents formally entertaining their guest. Her mother would have prepared a tasty meal for him, and Alison would have made sure the table appointments were just so. Frenchmen thought a lot of food, didn't they? Herself, she preferred a crust in congenial company, and that Marcel de Savigny was not. She recalled his slim athletic figure astride the great black horse. He was rather nice to look at, she had to concede that, but his arrogant air, his cold blue eyes, had antagonised her. It would take a cleverer woman than Alison to capture him, she considered, and she hoped her sister would not get hurt. Frenchmen talked a lot about *l'amour*, but when it came to marriage they were very businesslike, though her father *might* offer Lucifer as a dower. She thought that unlikely.

Then Terry came roaring into the yard on his new Honda, making the horses snort, and Jo's reflections were scattered like chaff before the wind, as she ran to greet him.

Terry Robinson was, from what could be discerned

under his mass of untidy hair, a good-looking young man. Periodically he tried to grow a beard, and then shaved it off. At that moment he wore long sideburns and a few straggles on his chin, which did not enhance his appearance. Although the day was warm he wore a scuffed leather jacket and frayed jeans. Involuntarily Jo recalled the Frenchman's spruce grooming, then dismissed the comparison with contempt. Terry was genuine without airs or affectation, he dressed to show his scorn for the conventions and established mores.

She dutifully admired the motorcycle and listened to Terry's enthusiastic description of its performance. He would take her out on it in the near future. She was his current 'bird' and he liked to have an admiring female in tow. She never minded travelling on his pillion in all weathers and was lavish in her praise of his machine and his prowess. Only rarely, and that was usually after a late night and a few beers, did he become amorous, but Jo did not encourage him. Sexually she was completely unawakened and was loud in her derision of what she called 'slop'. She found her life entirely satisfactory without plunging into emotional turmoils which might prove embarrassing. Terry laughed at her virginal recoil from his advances, hinted darkly that she would in time desire what she now scorned, but made no serious attempt to arouse her womanhood. He liked being seen about with her, but he was not in love with her.

When he had gone, Jo saddled Bonny and spent a blissful hour or so in the pasture field taking her over the jumps that had been put up in it. Absorbed in schooling the mare, she forgot all about their French visitor until, having bedded down, fed and watered the three horses, which she found far more interesting than any males, she came into the house to change for dinner. This was the only formality her father insisted upon.

'You can look as scruffy as you like during the day, but I require you to appear like civilised beings for our evening meal,' was what he told them, except for haysel and harvest, when they sometimes had to work until dark and the rule was waived.

Jo came in a little late to find Alison in the kitchen already changed, her evening dress covered by an overall, as she helped give the finishing touches to the dishes.

'For heaven's sake get a move on,' she said to Jo, eyeing her with disgust as she scattered hayseeds on the spotless tiles. 'Dinner will be on the table in fifteen minutes, and just look at you!'

'Oh, it won't take me a minute to change.' Jo pulled off her wellingtons, leaving them by the back door, and pattered across the floor on stockinged feet.

'Make yourself look respectable,' Alison called after her. 'In case you've forgotten, we have a guest.'

The immaculate Frenchman who had called her '*mon garçon*'. Reminded of the episode of the morning, Jo ran up the back stairs, grinning to herself, as her fingers turned the two fifty-pence coins in her pocket. Monsieur de Savigny had a little surprise coming to him and she was expecting to put him out of countenance.

Her room was at the end of the house, a low-ceilinged little apartment, beneath the window of which was the branch of a pear tree trained against the side of the house. As Jo kept her window open except in very bad weather, it was used as a means of exit and entrance by the farm cats. Devoted to all animals, Jo never minded their trespassing.

She dressed herself with unaccustomed care, for she

rarely wasted much time upon her toilet. She had a
quick shower and put on tights and underwear, followed by a blue linen dress with short sleeves and
square neckline. She brushed her chestnut hair until it
shone, and fastened round her throat the silver cross
and chain she had been given at her confirmation. She
rarely used cosmetics, and hesitated, lipstick in hand—
Alison had given her one on her last birthday—and
finally as the bell announcing dinner pealed through the
house, lightly touched her mouth with it, adding a layer
of powder to her freckled nose, most of which she
wiped off again.

She ran lightly down the front stairs, through the
arch behind them leading to the passage, and paused in
the entrance to the dining room. They were all there,
her mother at the head of the table, her father at the
foot, the guest on her mother's right hand, with Alison
next to him, her own place laid opposite to him, with
Jess beside it. It occurred to her then that the Thorntons were a very good-looking family, for her father
was still a handsome man, his hair the colour of hers,
showing just a tinge of grey, her mother pretty, if a little
faded, and Alison, in a filmy evening gown of dark wine
colour, which showed up her white skin but was most
unsuitable for a farmhouse, was nearly beautiful. It
seemed Marcel de Savigny thought so, for his dark head
was bent towards her and from her sister's smug expression he was paying her compliments. He, of course, was
immaculately clad in a dark suit, of some fine material,
perfectly tailored, a silk shirt and dark tie, gold cuf-
flinks visible when he moved his wrists, and gold watch
bracelet. The thin lips in the olive face had a satirical
twist, as if denying the sincerity of what he was saying.
Jo had a full view of him from where she was standing,

and her thought was how could Alison be such a fool as to lap up his nonsense. Long black lashes veiled the sapphire eyes, which she felt would be more revealing of his real thoughts.

Jo slid round behind her father's chair and into her place with a mumbled apology for being late.

'Just in time,' her father told her, 'I'm just beginning to carve.'

There was a succulent piece of beef in front of him, and the vegetable dishes were set before her mother. A good, plain English meal, including Yorkshire pudding.

Her mother said:

'I don't think you've met my middle daughter, Mr de Savigny. She was out last night when you arrived.'

Marcel gave her a perfunctory glance, seemingly absorbed in Alison.

'Enchanted to meet you, *mademoiselle*.'

'The name is Jo,' she informed him. 'Short for Josephine. And we've met before, Mr de Savigny.'

This time he did look at her more closely. His glance lingered on her bright head, the delicate contours of face and neck, the generous mouth with its hint of passion, and the big grey eyes which met his with impish glee.

'Where, Mademoiselle Jo? I've no recollection, and I'm sure I could not forget such a pretty face.'

Flowery! she thought disdainfully. I'm not pretty, not like Alison, she may mop up that sort of talk, but I believe he's laughing at us for being so unsophisticated. That we may be, but he wasn't exactly gallant this morning when he didn't know who I was.

'I didn't look very pretty this morning,' she admitted sweetly. 'My old sweater and jeans were not exactly Rue de la Paix, but I saddled Lucifer for you and you graciously gave me a tip.'

She fumbled in her pocket—she insisted that all her dresses should have pockets—and drew out the two silver coins. These she laid on the table in front of him.

Marcel stared at them, and then back at her, his expression incredulous.

'*Mon Dieu*, it is not possible you were *ce garçon-là*?'

'Reckon Oi was and all, bor,' she said in the vernacular.

CHAPTER TWO

Jo was uncertain how Marcel would react to her disclosure, but she anticipated that he would be abashed, especially if he recalled his coarse joke about the stallion. She wondered if she dared obliquely refer to it. Naturally he was at first surprised, and she waited eagerly for his next words, which must at least be an apology, but before he spoke her father gave her a suspicious look and demanded;

'What mischief have you been up to, Jo?'

'Mischief?' Jo contrived to look outraged. 'I was merely doing my usual morning's work, and you can't look glamorous when you're mucking out a stable.' She threw a glance at Marcel from under her long lashes. 'You must admit I'm an efficient groom.'

'Really, Jo,' Alison cut in severely, 'you should have introduced yourself properly. You can't blame Mr Savigny for taking you for a yokel, the sight you make of yourself.' She turned to Marcel with a placating smile. 'My sister is a bit of a hoyden, Mr de Savigny, she should beg your pardon for trying to embarrass you.'

'Are you embarrassed?' Jo asked hopefully.

But Marcel did not look at all disconcerted, he was smiling with genuine amusement and his blue eyes were twinkling.

'Why should I be?' he returned. 'Misled by your appearance and occupation, I made a very understandable mistake which you made no attempt to rectify, and you

23

obtained a *pourboire* under false pretences.' He stretched out a hand and picked up the coins. 'I don't pay for service from my hosts, I expect it to be given gratis.'

Jo flushed and bit back an angry retort; her joke had misfired and earned her a reprimand. She said sullenly:

'Perhaps you're shortsighted.'

'Not at all, but you could hardly expect me to detect feminine curves beneath that ... er ... voluminous sweater.' He looked pointedly at the slight swell of her breast revealed by the bodice of her dress. 'Such a charming figure too!'

Jo threw him a glance of pure hate. 'I've always wanted to be a boy.'

'Boy's clothes will not make you one, and if I had known your sex, I would have much preferred to saddle the colt myself.'

Jo flared up. 'If that isn't a case of sex discrimination ...'

Her father interrupted her. 'That will do, Jo.' He smiled at his guest. 'Jo tries to make up for the son I wanted, but now I've got her, I wouldn't want her changed.'

'Not when she makes such a delightful girl.'

'Oh, stuff!' Jo exclaimed rudely, as her father handed her a plate of beef. 'Be honest, Mr de Savigny, I'd prefer it. You think I'm anything but delightful.'

Marcel gave her a quizzical look, as he received his plate, which Annette loaded with vegetables. 'You cannot read my thoughts,' he told her, and addressed his host. 'You are to be congratulated, *mon ami*, on a trio of charming daughters.'

Insincere, Jo thought scornfully. Whatever Alison was doing, she had not tried to charm him.

Roger was pleased by the compliment, and recommended the sirloin he was carving to his guest.

'The famous English roast beef? It looks most appetising. But must we be so formal? My name is Marcel and I would be honoured if you will all call me by it.'

Jo attacked her dinner with gusto, but Alison toyed with hers as if she feared a display of healthy appetite was unfeminine. In response to Marcel's request, she said dimpling:

'If you'll do likewise. I think you know my name is Alison, not Ally as these wretched girls will call me.'

'Aleeson?' He drew out the middle syllable. 'Very pretty.' He looked across the table. 'Josephine and Jessica? Is that right?'

'Except that I like to be called Jo,' that lady stated.

'Because it sounds more masculine?'

'Not at all. Josephine is such a mouthful.'

'It is a beautiful name. We had an Empress called by it.'

'The one that got herself divorced.'

Alison frowned at her sister's tone. 'For reasons of state.'

'Oh, come off it, Ally, it was because she couldn't give Napoleon a son and heir. I'd expect my husband to stick to me, even if I was barren.'

Alison turned to Marcel apologetically. 'You must forgive my sister, she spends so much time with the farmhands she's becoming a little uncouth.'

' I like plain speaking,' Marcel said gallantly.

'Don't encourage her,' Jess warned him, 'or you'll get more than you bargained for.' She winked at Jo.

Marcel sent Jo a challenging glance across the table.

'I can cope with her,' he said confidently.

Feeling Jo was being made too important, Alison

diverted his attention, and the conversation became general. Taking no part in it, Jo surreptitiously studied the face opposite to her, which attracted her in spite of herself. It was thin and aquiline, the mouth narrow-lipped above a firm chin. His black brows were slightly slanted above the keen blue eyes. His dark head was set proudly upon broad shoulders, and in his well tailored suit he looked every inch an aristocrat. A man born to rule, and since his father was dead, he probably did rule his family and estate with a strong hand. Not a man it would be wise to thwart, she thought involuntarily. Contrarily she resolved to oppose him in every way possible; he should never dictate to her.

Roast beef was followed by apple pie and cream, the two younger girls changing the plates and dishes. Alison hastily checked Marcel's movement to assist.

'It's their chore,' she told him, 'they always do it. I suppose you've lots of servants to wait on you at your château?'

'Too many,' he replied. 'But my grandmother lives with us, and she clings to the old ways, though I prefer informality myself.'

'We can't get anyone to live in here,' Mrs Thornton explained. 'Girls won't go into service, as they call it, if they can get anything else to do.'

'Why should I pay exorbitant wages for indifferent service when I've three girls at home doing nothing?' her husband asked, which remark brought forth indignant protests from his family, all declaring that they had many tasks to fill their day.

'Until you get husbands,' Marcel suggested with a sly glance at Alison.

'I shall never marry,' Jo declared firmly. 'Alison will, of course, as soon as anyone asks her. We don't know yet how Jess is going to turn out, but I only want to stay on the farm all my days. I can't believe I'll ever find a husband more interesting than a horse.'

An assertion which produced laughter and teasing and provoked Marcel's interest. Jo became aware that he was watching her out of the corner of his eye while he talked to Alison. She found his blue gaze embarrassing, and would have been furious if she had guessed his thoughts. She might try to ape a boy, but his experienced eyes saw the potential of the passionate woman she would one day become. No Latin girl of her age could ever be so completely unaware of sex, as she was, but the signs were there in her face, and the full curve of her lower lip. Alison was pretty, but shallow; this young sister of hers would be beautiful and had depths in her which would be exciting to plumb, once she was awakened. Marcel usually avoided young girls, they too easily became intense, and adolescent adoration bored him, but Josephine Thornton intrigued him.

'Tomorrow is market day,' Roger Thornton was saying. 'I'll be away all morning, and you wouldn't be interested, my boy. Jo, you can take Marcel riding in the forest, he hasn't been there yet.'

'Oh, no, I can't,' Jo was dismayed at the prospect. 'I've my work to do.'

'What work? You'll be finished in the stables by breakfast time, and the horses need exercise. We haven't started to cut hay yet.'

'You're being discourteous, Jo,' Alison scolded her. 'If only I could ride, I'd love to come with you, Marcel, but unfortunately I'm allergic to horses.'

But Marcel's eyes were fixed upon Jo.

'Are you still annoyed with me because I took you for a stable-boy?' he asked.

Jessica laughed. 'She can't blame you for that. She looks a proper mess when she's grooming the horses.'

'I hope you'll smarten yourself up a bit before you go riding with Marcel, or he'll be ashamed to be seen with you,' Alison said nastily.

'I could never be that,' Marcel assured her politely. 'Mademoiselle Josephine, will you honour me by accompanying me tomorrow morning?'

'Oh, very well,' Jo agreed ungraciously, needled by her sisters' remarks. 'I promise you that both I and the horses will be immaculate.'

She met his blue eyes with a hint of challenge in her clear grey eyes. She was determined to show him she could appear as well turned out as any of his country-women.

'I'm sure you will,' he responded, and raised his wine glass. 'Here's to our ripening acquaintanceship, *mon garçon*.'

'An *entente cordiale*?' she suggested archly.

'Quite so.'

'What exactly does that mean?' Jess enquired.

'Reciprocity between English and French.'

Which was not Jo's intention at all.

True to her promise, she had both horses beautifully groomed, even going to the trouble of polishing their hooves by nine o'clock, which was the after-breakfast hour Marcel had chosen for their expedition. With her own appearance she was not quite so successful. Her jodhpurs were worn, she was due for a new pair before the summer gymkhanas, and the shirt she wore in pre-ference to a hacking jacket, which would be hot, was faded though clean. Her riding hat obscured the glory of her hair. Marcel came to join her again in well cut riding breeches and boots, his peaked cap shading his eyes. In his gloved hand he carried a riding crop.

'Punctual to the minute,' he exclaimed, glancing at his watch. They had not yet met that morning, for Jo had eaten long before he did.

'I always am,' Jo returned. 'I can't afford to waste time dawdling like fashionable ladies do.'

'Being of course familiar with the breed,' he taunted as he took hold of Captain's reins.

Jo flushed. 'I've read about them,' she snapped.

'Secondhand knowledge is often inaccurate,' he told her, swinging himself into the saddle. Jo mounted Bonny and pointed to his riding crop.

'You won't need that. I never use one.'

'I do not either, but it gives me . . . confidence.'

He didn't need anything to give him that, Jo thought, more likely he carried it for show. He had not made the mistake of trying to assist her to mount—that she would have resented furiously. Since he lived in a château, she had taken it for granted the women of his household would be society ladies, but she did not know how many there were; he had only mentioned a grandmother.

Captain was very fresh and waltzed round the yard. He tried to buck, but was quickly forestalled; he then attempted to set off at a gallop but was firmly restrained. Jo could not fault Marcel's horsemanship, though she did not like the man. Intuitively she felt he could be a threat to her independence.

Since he did not know the way, Jo went first, trotting across a pasture field behind the farm. She paused to open a gate expertly without dismounting, and gave the grey a wide berth as he went through, pulling the gate shut behind him. They were on an expanse of common and she said tersely:

'You can give him his head now,' and urged her mount to a gallop.

Captain soon overtook her and they raced neck and neck until they reached the forest. They had to reduce their speed as they entered a long green ride. Trees, mostly conifers, were closely grouped on either side of them, with shadowy depths between them which, when much younger, Jo had imaginatively peopled with wolves and bears. They looked sinister enough for such inhabitants, though they harboured nothing fiercer than rabbits, weasels and an occasional fox.

'The trees grow taller in my country,' Marcel told her.

'I've no doubt everything is bigger and better,' Jo returned, sarcastically. 'I've never been abroad, and England's good enough for me.'

Marcel gave her a sharp look, seeming about to rebuke her, but checked himself. He reined in to allow her to precede him, as she took a turn off the ride that led down into a glade where deciduous trees predominated and a little stream ran through it. Here the foliage was all shades of green, and wild roses threw delicate sprays of tinted blossom over mounds and stumps, with here and there a stand of honeysuckle perfuming the air. Ascending a steep path, they came out upon a different scene. A field, enclosed on three sides by the forest, was bright with young corn dotted with scarlet poppies, and edged with masses of golden broom. On the fourth and open side was a view of further cultivated fields and a farmhouse.

'Let us pause here,' said Marcel, and slid from his horse.

'Want to admire the view?' Jo enquired without dismounting. Surely he could not be feeling tired?

Marcel indicated a fallen tree trunk. 'A place to sit,' he suggested. 'This is a delightful spot, and I could do with a smoke.'

'I'm glad you approve of it,' Jo said disagreeably, and unwillingly descended from her horse. Marcel took Bonny's reins and secured both horses to a tree. Then he sat down on the log, obviously expecting her to do likewise. She did so, sitting as far apart from him as the trunk permitted. He gave her a quizzical look and offered her his cigarette case.

'No, thank you, I don't smoke.'

She noticed the case was silver and bore a coat of arms.

'I only do very rarely.' He pocketed the case and produced a packet of small cheroots. The aromatic blue smoke from the one he lit rose in the still air. Jo crossed her legs and clasped her knee with her hands, her eyes fixed on the distant farm, trying to dissociate herself from her companion. He was having an oddly disturbing effect upon her, for she was almost painfully conscious of his proximity. In spite of his trim elegance, he was a very masculine man, and deep within her, her latent femininity stirred in response.

All around them, nature was busy with the business of reproduction. Birds flew back and forth feeding their rapacious young, bees gathered honey from foxgloves and harebells growing beside the path to replenish their hives, though spring and the mating season were past, the forest was burgeoning with new life. Jo became aware that Marcel had turned his lean brown face towards her and was studying her with disconcerting blue eyes.

'You intrigue me, Josephine,' he said softly. 'You have the makings of a desirable woman and yet you try to ape a boy. Why?'

'I should have been a boy,' she tried to explain. 'Daddy wanted a son, but he's been unlucky. So I've tried to make up to him for my sex. Girls are as efficient as men nowadays, and I aim to be as good a farmer as a boy would have been.'

He made a gesture of distaste. 'It is no life for a woman.'

She met his gaze with candid grey eyes.

'It's the life I want. I'm not drawn to being a wife and mother, though I might marry if the right man comes along. One who could help run the farm.'

'You put that first?'

'Of course. It's essential if Greyfriars is to carry on as a going concern.'

'Have you anyone in view for this secondary position?'

She laughed merrily. 'Not yet, but there's plenty of time. I'm only nineteen, you know.'

'Girls begin to think about love and romance much younger than that nowadays.'

'I know they do, but I've no time for that sort of nonsense,' Jo declared blithely. 'I leave romance to Alison, who hates farm work. I ride at the local shows, you know, and ... and ... I've dreams of becoming a show-jumper.' She blushed charmingly and wondered why she was unburdening herself to this stranger. Her future could be of no interest to him.

'No!' Marcel exclaimed vehemently. 'That is all wrong. You are not the hardbitten, horsey type. Your dreams should be of a very different future.'

Jo unclasped her hands and straightened herself.

'You think they should be of some man?' she said scornfully. 'Once and for all, Mr de Savigny, I'm not and never will be one of your soppy feminine women, though your masculine vanity may find that hard to believe!'

Marcel laughed deep in his throat, a sound that stirred her inexplicably.

'So very young and naïve in spite of your nineteen years! But beware, Josephine, you have not got that passionate mouth for nothing. Sooner or later your womanhood will catch up with you.'

Jo coloured furiously. 'Oh, stuff!' she muttered.

'You're a challenge to a mere male, and I am half inclined to take you up on it.'

She saw the glint in his eyes, and shrank back as he rose to his feet.

'What . . . what do you mean, Marcel?'

'I will show you.'

Before she could guess his intention, he had caught both her hands in his and pulled her up on to her feet and into his arms. She flinched like a startled filly, and her eyelids drooped before the sudden flame in his eyes. Then very deliberately he tightened his hold until she was pressed against him, and his mouth descended upon hers.

A quiver ran through her body and she relaxed in his embrace, confused by the rapid beating of her heart, and a new emotion that was strange to her. His kiss was long and close, arousing strange sensations, until a wave of virginal recoil swept through her and she wrenched herself out of his arms.

'How dare you!'

He laughed mockingly. 'Not a very original response.'

Her hand flew to her outraged lips. 'You . . . you cad!'

'Haven't you been kissed before?'

Her mind recalled Terry.

'My boy-friend tries occasionally, but I don't like it.'

'So you have got a *bien-aimé*? Tell me about him.'

Carelessly spoken yet with an intentness of regard that suggested his interest was more than perfunctory, but Jo was too bewildered by her reactions to notice.

'He's not a lover, if that's what you're thinking,' she assured him. 'He's a guy I picked up at a disco, and we think alike about most things, and he's got a super motorbike.'

Marcel's thin lips curled disparagingly.

'You ride on his pillion?'

'Of course. He won't let me try solo, at least not yet. I'll get round him in the end.'

'A most dangerous and unsuitable proceeding,' Marcel commented.

'Danger gives a spice to living,' she retorted.

'Ah, I am with you there, but there are other forms with less risk to life and limb.'

Again there was a glint in his eyes as he moved towards her, and Jo's pulse quickened. Dimly she was aware that there were forces within him which could move her to a response she did not want to give. Hastily she backed away from him.

'If you want to play those sort of games, why don't you pick someone of your own age?' she demanded. 'Not someone young and naïve as you say I am.'

'Because I prefer an unformed mould which I can shape to my liking.'

Jo's eyes widened. 'Of all the arrogant cheek!'

'Why so? It is sensible. Frenchmen usually marry much younger wives. The husband should be the dominant partner and then there is less chance of friction.'

'Alison isn't a doormat,' Jo remarked with apparent irrelevance. The mention of wives had turned her thoughts towards her sister, who she knew was much taken with their visitor.

'She is charming,' Marcel raised his brows. 'But I fail to see the connection.'

'Then you're dimmer than I thought,' Jo returned. She sat down on the log again, determined to clear up Marcel's position with regard to Alison's hopes.

'I suppose being French you still have arranged marriages. Are you engaged?'

'No. It is true my parents sought to betroth me in my cradle, but I rejected their choice. They are both dead now, so I do not need to consult their wishes.'

'So you're an orphan,' Jo said slowly. 'I'm sorry, Marcel.'

'You need not be. I did not get on with my father and my mother was a fashionable doll without a heart. But I am not alone in the world. I have a grandmother whom I love and respect, and a young sister who is something of a responsibility.'

'What an odd household!' Jo was wondering if Alison could fit into it.

'We are not all blessed with united families like yours.'

'I suppose we're lucky, and mine is connected with yours.' Jo assumed a quaintly adult air, which diverted her companion exceedingly. 'It seems to me you need a wife, and Alison would suit you very well. You wouldn't have to mould and shape her, she'd run your château beautifully and she prefers older men.'

Yet even while she sought to promote her sister's cause, she felt an inexplicable envy, which was absurd; Marcel's way of life was not for her.

'Thank you for planning my future.' Marcel was very dry. 'It seems you are feminine enough to indulge in matchmaking, but I am capable of doing my own wooing. Might I point out that older men have their points, they are usually established and have more experience, but it seems your preference is for callow drop-outs like Terry Robinson.'

Jo's eyes flashed. 'Don't you call him names, you know nothing about him!'

'Enough to know he is not a suitable companion for you.'

'Ally, I suppose,' Jo surmised. 'She doesn't like him because he has long hair and advanced ideas.'

'It is your father who does not approve of the connection.'

'So you've been discussing my affairs with him? How dare you—they're nothing to do with you!'

'But if I married into your family they would be,' Marcel said silkily. 'I am very particular about my sister's male companions.'

Jo's eyes flashed again. 'You're a tyrannical snob, Mr de Savigny, and if you imagine Jess and I will allow you to censor our friendships you're making a big mistake. Daddy says your ancestors were *comtes*, but you won't have any *droit du seigneur* over us!'

Marcel laughed heartily and Jo flushed, realising she had blundered.

'Do you know what that means?' he asked when his merriment had subsided.

'Right to something or other,' she muttered sullenly.

'Right to the first night with a tenant's bride,' Marcel informed her.

'Oh!' Jo's colour deepened. 'Of course I didn't mean that. Your ancestors must have been a dirty lot if they did that.'

'They only very rarely availed themselves of the privilege.'

'I should hope not. No wonder there was a revolution!'

'That is all old history. To return to the present day—if you desire initiation,' the blue eyes glinted wickedly, 'I could supply you with a more suitable teacher than Terry Robinson.'

Jo sprang to her feet. 'How dare you make such nasty insinuations!' she cried furiously. 'Terry's all right, and we don't want you around bossing our lives. Who do you think you are? A sort of god?'

'Nothing so impressive, but I do know how to deal with rude teenagers,' he retorted.

He reached for her before she could evade him and, sitting down again, pulled her across his knees. His eyes were alight with mischievous enjoyment as she struggled to free herself.

'The mere male still has the advantage of superior physical strength,' he remarked. 'Are you going to apologise?'

'What for? Let me go, you horrible brute!'

He was strong. Though she was no weakling, she was quite helpless in her ignominious position.

'Charming little *derrière* you have,' Marcel said admiringly, 'but you are a little old to be spanked. You pretend not to like being kissed, but your response just now was adequate if a trifle amateurish. Shall we repeat the performance and you might acquire a taste for it?'

Jo squirmed and muttered: 'See you damned first!'

But Marcel only laughed.

'What an unladylike pronouncement! *Ma chère* Josephine, do try to be a little more sophisticated. This place cries out for amorous dalliance.'

He turned her over and bent his head, seeking her lips. Jo made a convulsive movement, and they both rolled off the log, with Marcel on top of her. Then something happened that neither had expected. It was as if a flame had suddenly ignited between them. His hard, lean body was pressing hers into the moss below the tree trunk, and Jo's arms of their own volition went about his neck. His mouth was on hers, then on her throat, her neck, while wave upon wave of excitement pulsed through her. When eventually Marcel stood up, Jo lay quivering at his feet, striving to contend with the storm of emotion he had aroused in her. She had lost her hat and her hair was sprayed about her neck and shoulders, while her small breasts heaved beneath her torn shirt, for both were breathing fast, but Marcel recovered first. He looked down at her recumbent body and a faint compunction showed in his eyes.

'So young and so vulnerable,' he said softly.

Jo raised herself on her hands and stared up at his dark face with wide, indignant eyes. She had an unhappy suspicion that she had clung to him and her mouth had opened under his. How could she have so demeaned herself? Amorous dalliance, he had called it, and no doubt he acted so with every available woman. She was as angry with herself for yielding to him as she was with him.

Marcel bent towards her, holding out his hand.

'Let me help you up—I am afraid I have torn your shirt.'

Blind fury swept through her, swamping all other feelings. She struck his hand aside and sprang to her feet, pulling her shirt together over her slight bosom, recalling that the devil had actually kissed her breasts.

'If you wanted to punish me for being impertinent, I'd much rather you'd beaten me!' she snapped.

'I may be provoked into doing that if you aren't more civil, but I find it more amusing to teach you to become a woman.'

'Oh, you . . . you . . !' she raged.

Marcel laughed.

'You show every sign of being an apt pupil—there is plenty of passion in you, you are no icicle.'

Jo took a step forward, wanting to hit him, and her foot touched his riding crop which he had dropped on the ground when he had sat down. Quick as thought she snatched it up and struck him across his mocking face. Then without waiting to see what damage she had done, she fled towards the tethered horses. She loosed them both, and as the startled grey snorted and reared, swung herself on to the more placid Bonny's back and galloped recklessly down the woodland track as if all the devils in hell were in pursuit of her.

CHAPTER THREE

ONCE clear of the forest, Jo slowed her sweating mount to a walk and began to have misgivings. She had expected Captain to follow her, in which case Marcel would have a long walk home, which she considered was no more than he deserved. But there was no sign of the grey behind her and it occurred to her that he might have become caught up in his loose reins and injured himself, a possibility which troubled her. On the other hand, Marcel might have been able to catch him, in which event he could be hard upon her heels, and she glanced nervously at the entrance to the forest, increasing Bonny's pace to a trot.

How she was to account for her return alone, she did not know, but fortunately Roger would not be back from the market until late afternoon, by which time Marcel and/or the horse should have put in an appearance. She was loath to tell her father what had happened in the forest, which was her excuse for her conduct. The recollection caused her to go hot with shame. But Roger would require some explanation as to why his guest and his gelding were missing. He might not believe that Marcel had made a pass at her, for up to now he had only shown an interest in Alison, and to have to confess that Marcel had administered what he considered a well deserved chastisement would be too humiliating. Jo felt a resurgence of fury as she recalled his methods.

He had not had it all his own way, she knew she must

have marked him, but he could retaliate, for her father would believe what he chose to tell him. Only a charge of attempted seduction could justify what she had done, but that had not been Marcel's intention, and he would laugh at her for so misinterpreting his actions, for if it had been, he would not have stopped when he did. If he admitted that he had kissed her at all, he would declare she must be naïve if she construed a few kisses as intended rape. In retrospect the whole episode seemed so unlikely that her relatives would believe she was accusing him for a mischievous prank which she had followed up by deserting him. No, it would not be easy to explain what she had done.

Jo was tempted to ride away and seek asylum at one of the other farms where she had friends until the storm had blown over, but her conscience was troubled about Captain's fate, and she knew someone ought to go to look for him. She dared not, in case she encountered an outraged Marcel, but Bert might be persuaded to hunt for him if he were not busy.

She rode into the yard, and as she did so, her father emerged from the barn and she realised with dismay that he had returned early, instead of staying to lunch with his colleagues as he usually did, possibly on Marcel's account. What on earth was she going to say to him?

He came up to her, frowning at Bonny's still heaving flanks and Jo's windblown hair.

'She's all in a lather, and you've lost your hat. Has something happened, Jo?'

'Nothing much,' Jo mumbled as she slid to the ground. 'Bonny bolted with me and I couldn't hold her, and my hat was blown off.'

She had left it in the forest glade where she had sat

with Marcel, and it added to her irritation that she had lost a nearly new one.

'Did something frighten her?' Roger looked concerned.

'I . . . yes, it did.' Jo began to improvise wildly. 'A pheasant flew up suddenly and startled her—you know what a noise they make.'

Roger stroked the mare's sweat-soaked neck.

'You'd better rub her down. Where's Marcel?'

This was the question she had dreaded.

'I don't know,' she said truthfully. 'He was following, but he wouldn't want to override Captain trying to catch up with me. Perhaps he's lost his way.'

'I'd better go and look for him.'

Jo quailed. What might her father find in the forest?

'He can ask someone to direct him, surely,' she said hurriedly. 'He wouldn't have to go far without coming upon a house or a cottage.'

'That's so.' Roger sounded relieved. 'Ah, here he is.'

Jo looked round as Marcel rode into the yard looking as cool and debonair as if nothing had happened. But there was a red weal across his face from his forehead, over the bridge of his nose and down one cheek. She gave a little gasp as she saw her handiwork; she had not meant to mark him so badly. She was relieved to see Captain was safe, but how was Marcel going to explain his injury? There was an inimical gleam in his eyes as he looked at her.

'What on earth have you done to your face?' Roger demanded.

Marcel smiled faintly as he touched the angry mark.

'The trees in your forest have some low branches. I rode into one.'

Jo drew a long breath of relief. He was not going to give her away.

'I suppose that was after Jo left you?' Roger enquired. 'She says Bonny bolted and in your anxiety for her you can't have been looking where you were going.'

'Exactly so,' Marcel confirmed drily. 'I see she has returned safely.'

'You were a long way behind her,' Roger went on. He was no fool and he had sensed the tension between the pair of them. There was something here he did not understand. 'We feared you'd lost your way.'

'No, I didn't do that,' Marcel told him coolly, 'but Captain ... er ... jibbed a bit.' He dismounted and patted the horse.

'Funny, I've never known him do that,' Roger declared.

'Perhaps he doesn't like foreigners,' Marcel suggested, and his eyes met Jo's. She was struggling with an unwelcome feeling of contrition, wishing that she had not struck so hard. There was a hard glitter in his blue gaze and though he was making light of the incident, she knew she was not going to be forgiven.

'He backed into a bramble bush,' Marcel went on. 'He has got a few scratches, I am afraid, but nothing serious.'

He was still looking at Jo and because she knew she was to blame for Captain's mishap, her feeling of guilt increased.

'Humph.' Roger was looking at the horse's legs. 'Jo, you'd better put something on them.' He straightened himself. 'A pity Bonny bolted.'

'Was it not?' Marcel agreed suavely. '*Alors*, Josephine, these beasts need attention.'

Jo led Bonny into her stall, and Marcel, following her, took Captain into the adjacent one. As she removed the mare's saddle he called to her:

'As your father said, I need some salve or embrocation. This animal has cut himself. Can you find some?'

Jo put the saddle on its peg and ran into the tack

room next door where they kept a medicine chest. She stood by Captain's head stroking his nose while Marcel applied the ointment, but the horse was quiet under his ministrations. She knew he would never have jibbed while Marcel rode him. She was deeply concerned, because she had broken her code, which was that no pain or injury should be inflicted upon an animal through carelessness or neglect. She had overlooked the danger to Captain when she had turned him loose.

'*Eh bien*, he will do,' said Marcel as he completed his task. He looked at Jo severely. 'It is no thanks to you it was not much worse. He had got himself caught up by his reins, and a frightened horse can do itself a lot of damage.'

Jo hung her head. 'I . . . I didn't think . . .'

'Then do so before you contemplate any further rashness. You also left your hat behind you, but I retrieved it. I put it on the gatepost in case it provoked questions if I came in carrying it.'

'That was very thoughtful of you.'

'*N'importe*.' He left the stall and she followed him, calling his name as he reached the doorway.

'Yes?'

'Can't I do something about your face? Bathe it, perhaps?'

'No, thank you, you might do more damage.'

'I . . . I'm sorry, Marcel, I didn't mean to hit so hard.'

He looked her up and down with a sardonic smile, but when he spoke his voice was clipped and curt.

'If you were the boy you like to pretend you are, I would give you the thrashing you deserve, but since you are a girl, I shall have to devise a more subtle punishment.'

'I thought you'd already administered that,' Jo cried,

flushing angrily. She pointed to the weal. 'That was a reprisal for what you did to me. I take back my apology. I wish I'd hit you harder!'

'If you had the penalty would be that much greater.'

'I suppose such threats soothe your wounded dignity,' Jo said loftily, 'but I'll take darned good care you don't get me alone again.' Actually there was no one else in the stable, but her father was within call in the yard. 'It's you who should be apologising for your shocking behaviour.'

'Which you enjoyed.'

Jo's grey eyes blazed. 'Never! I'd sooner be mauled by a . . . a . . .'

'Gorilla?' he suggested, 'but the simile would not be very apt. You were not exactly unresponsive in my arms, Josephine, but you have still a lot to learn about love, and it will give me great pleasure to further your education.'

'You flatter yourself, Mr de Savigny, and I may be an unsophisticated idiot, but I do know that what happened in the glade had nothing to do with love—that's different altogether. As for my further education, as you call it, you'll not get another opportunity.'

'Oh, but I shall,' he returned suavely. 'You can be quite sure of that.'

'Not in a month of Sundays!' Jo declared, and made a rude face at him.

Marcel laughed derisively, and gave the victory sign with his fingers. Then he strode away towards the house, whistling gaily as if he had not a care in the world. For all that, the mark on his face must be painful, she thought with satisfaction, her earlier regret completely forgotten. Nevertheless it was some time before she had sufficiently recovered herself to feed and water the horses. Marcel excited and disturbed her, and though she assured herself his threats were idle, mere salve for injured vanity; the thought of them being implemented caused a turmoil in her blood. Thank God he won't be here much longer, she consoled herself.

Jo felt she had had enough of Monsieur de Savigny for one day, and she shrank from sitting opposite to him that night with that mark upon his face troubling her conscience. Alison would be full of commiseration about his 'accident' and his rejoinders would be double-edged and aimed to make her feel uncomfortable, for she was ashamed of her violence, though she repeatedly told herself it was no more than he deserved. She decided she would try to arrange a date with Terry, and since her father was occupied with inspecting the hay-cutter, she went into his office to make her call where only Jess was present.

But Terry was not co-operative.

'You know I always like having you with me, but the fact is, I've got a date at the Pelican for tonight.'

'Another girl?' she asked in dismayed surprise, for she thought Terry was her exclusive property.

'Oh no, of course not, you're my bird, Jo, but ... well, the Pelican isn't considered a fit place for a nice girl.'

'Oh, rubbish, I don't believe it's as bad as it's made out to be, and *I'm* not a nice girl, I'm an adventurous one, and I can look after myself. What's the big attraction, anyway?'

'The Buccaneers will be performing, so it's rather special.'

'I'd love to hear them.' They were a well-known pop group. 'Please, Terry, do take me!'

He hedged a little, for he knew Mr Thornton would

be furious if he discovered he had taken his daughter to
such a place, and Roger did business with the Rob-
insons' garage. Moreover, evenings at the Pelican
usually ended in a rough-house, and though he was
eager for excitement himself, he did not want to be
hampered by a girl. But in the end he yielded to Jo's
pleading.

'Okay, Jo, I'll take you along, but if I'm not fit to
ride home we might have to spend the night under a
haystack.'

'That would be fun.'

'Would it?' he laughed. 'You're coming on, Jo, so
provided it isn't raining, we'll try it. I'll pick you up at
the usual time in the usual place. Be seeing you.'

He hung up. His suggestion of a haystack was a little
ambiguous, but Jo was confident she could handle him
if he became fresh, and she was elated at the prospect of
visiting the infamous Pelican.

'Got yourself a date?' Jess asked, looking up from the
farm accounts on which she was working.

'Yes, I'm going with Terry to the Pelican.'

Jess looked startled. 'You mustn't go there, Jo. Dad
wouldn't like it.'

'He doesn't like a lot of things I do, and I'm sure its
reputation has been exaggerated. I'm going to find out
for myself. You won't split on me?'

'Of course not, though I thinkk you're being rash.' Jess
looked admiringly at her sister. 'I believe you'd dare
anything for a kick.'

'I'm no chicken,' Jo boasted, 'and I can't come to any
harm with Terry there.'

She then suggested that as it was a lovely day they
took their lunch out into the fields, because Jess must
be fed up with stewing indoors. Her sister agreed, and

having raided the larder they set out for their picnic in a woodland grove adjoining the hayfield.

'How did you get on with Marcel this morning?' Jess enquired as they sprawled on the grass replete with ham, cheese and salad.

'Oh, all right,' Jo replied casually, but she could not meet her sister's eyes. 'How long is he staying?'

'Only for a week, I think, but he wants to take one of us back with him.'

Startled, Jo sat up abruptly. 'Oh lord, don't say he and Ally are engaged!'

'Not yet. What he told Daddy was that he wants one of us to be a sort of companion to his sister, and improve her English during her stay. They were discussing it before breakfast in here while I was opening the mail. I wish he'd take me.'

'I shouldn't think it would be much fun if his sister is anything like him.'

'But I like him,' Jess declared. 'He's so good-looking and amusing. I don't know what you've got against him.'

Jo looked at her with contemptuous pity.

'I suppose you've got a schoolgirl crush on him.'

'I've left school and I'm not ashamed of admiring him,' Jess declared heatedly. 'But of course he's only got eyes for Ally. I think the sister business is just an excuse to get her over there.'

Jo looked doubtful; she did not think Marcel's intentions were serious. Jess, who did, went on:

'If she pulls it off I suppose you, I and Thérèse, that's the sister would be bridesmaids, but I wish the wedding could be in France, then I'd see the château.'

'Got it all worked out, haven't you?' Jo told her scornfully. 'I don't want to be connected with the de

Savignys, and I wish that foreigner had never come here!'

She scrambled to her feet and walked away into the trees, while Jess stared after her in surprise, wondering what had come over her, and indeed Jo was puzzled about that herself. She was only aware that the thought of Marcel and Alison's wedding was repugnant to her, and decided it was because she felt certain Alison could not be happy with a man who behaved as he had done towards herself in the forest that morning, but Alison's happiness had never greatly concerned her, she believed her sister was well able to take care of herself, and she would not accept overtures from the Frenchman unless she was convinced he was serious. It's because I hate changes, Jo decided, and now we're grown up they're inevitable. Ally won't want to stay at home like I do all her life, nor will Jess. She felt restless and disturbed, as if the new life seeping into verdure and blossom all about her was echoing in her own blood. She too was changing and she resented the process.

She slipped out to meet Terry without telling anyone where she was going. Jess would tell them at dinner that she had an engagement, and they were quite used to her going off with Terry. She wore a new pair of black slacks with a tight black tee-shirt, that had a low neckline. The get-up made her look very slim, and black showed up the red in her hair. She wore no coat since it was a warm evening, and Terry had lent her a crash helmet which she carried.

Terry met her at the end of the drive up to the farm, which was their usual rendezvous. Jo thought he looked more unkempt than ever, or perhaps it was by contrast with Marcel. His hair could do with a wash and the bottoms of his jeans were frayed. His deliberate cult of sartorial shabbiness for the first time jarred upon her. He was frowning as she came up to him and began to raise further objections to taking her with him.

'You don't know what it'll be like.'

'That's what I want to find out,' she returned cheerfully. 'Go on, Terry, you can't disappoint me now.' The thought of facing Marcel across the dinner table recurred to her and added urgency to her plea. 'I'll begin to think you've got another girl you don't want me to meet.'

'I don't go with the sort who go to the Pelican,' he growled. 'That's just it.' He looked up and down her slim black-clad figure. 'You look too nice.'

Jo laughed. 'What's wrong, Terry? I'm sure my clothes are very ordinary, and after riding your bike, I shan't be too tidy when I get there.'

It was not her appearance, but her fresh, innocent face and trusting eyes that were giving him qualms.

'Ah, come on!' he capitulated. 'Hop on, it's getting late.'

Jo put on her helmet and scrambled on to the pillion, putting her arms round Terry's waist, as unselfconsciously as if he were another girl.

'You'll be there to protect me,' she said in his ear.

Terry grunted noncommittally. An evening spent protecting Jo was not what he wanted. The motorcycle roared away.

The Pelican was at some distance from the farm, amid a few scattered houses on a main road. A bracken-covered slope rose behind it, affording cover for lovers seeking privacy during the evening's entertainment. It was a one-storey timbered building and its present function, after a varied history, was as dance hall–cum-bar. Its front was decorated with coloured electric light bulbs, which made it look festive, but inside it presented a sleazy appearance, its walls lined with benches, and covered with out-of-date posters, the floor unscrubbed. A bar was at one end and a small platform at the other accommodated the musicians. The Buccaneers, in semi-piratical costumes, were a group on the way up and eager for any engagement, though actually the Pelican paid well.

Almost at once Jo wished she had not come. There was a gang of youths from the nearest big town, who were a rough crowd, and would become troublesome when the drink began to affect them, and the beer was flowing freely. The language they used was lurid. Although in her youthful arrogance Jo believed she was unshockable, she shrank from the spate of near-obscenity, and the over-painted young women, whom even her innocence recognised as tarts. Terry became excited by the music and drink. He tried to paw her and when she resisted, sulked, making frequent expeditions to the bar. There was a look in his eye which caused Jo apprehension. He had suggested a night out, and since it was obvious he would not be in a fit state to ride his motorcycle home, she feared he was anticipating sleeping with her under a haystack. She began to calculate the distance between the Pelican and Greyfriars, and surmised they had come between twenty and thirty miles. It would be a long walk alone at night.

When Terry had left her for yet another beer, a swaggering young tough accosted her with a demand that she accompany him outside. He was a handsome brute and used to having his own way with girls. Various couples had sought the seclusion of the bracken bank, and he had been attracted by Jo's aloof air, and as he told her, he had a fancy for coppernobs. But Jo did not fancy him and looked round anxiously for Terry, who came weaving towards them.

'Tha's my bird,' he mumbled.

Jo's new admirer had no intention of relinquishing her. Holding her by one wrist, he told Terry rudely to get lost, then as she protested, informed her:

'That baby face ain't no b—— good to you, he's only half weaned. You come along o' me.'

Jo's temper flared, and she wished she had Marcel's riding crop, she would have no scruple about marking this fellow's face. Fighting to free her wrist, she cried:

'Let me go, you great bully, I don't want anything to do with you!' With her free hand she clawed at his face.

He caught her other wrist and twisted her arms behind her, hurting her.

'Spitfire, you'll b—— well pay for that!'

'Terry! Please!' Jo cried desperately.

Several of the gang had come up to them, spoiling for a fight, and Terry shrank away from their threatening faces. Jo realised that he could not, or dared not, help her. The bartender was carefully looking the other way. She was dragged towards the entrance, when the door was flung open and Marcel de Savigny stood on the threshold. Had the Angel Gabriel suddenly appeared to succour her Jo could not have been more astonished, or more shamed. That he should have come upon her in such a predicament! The group round the entrance were also surprised; well-dressed, and elegant, Marcel looked like a being from another planet. He said suavely:

'Kindly let the young lady go.'

The youth had slackened his grip on Jo's arms, and she twisted free, running to her rescuer, who told her curtly:

'Get into the car, it's at the door.'

'No, you don't.' The youth was not going to allow his prey to escape so easily. 'You b—— well keep out of this, mister, or I'll spoil that pretty face of yours!' And Jo, to her horror, caught the glint of a flick-knife.

Marcel aimed a blow at the youth's chin and he went down like a felled ox.

His comrades, seeing their leader drop, hesitated, and Marcel pushed Jo through the door and slammed it in their faces. He almost threw her into the car, and whisked round to get into the driver's seat, as with howls of rage the young hooligans came pouring out of the hall. The car shot forward, pursued by a fusillade of small stones, none of which hit it.

'We must go back,' Jo cried, wrestling with the door handle. 'They'll kill Terry!'

'Sit still and leave that alone,' Marcel commanded. He freed one hand from the wheel and jerked her back in her seat. 'Do you want to kill yourself? He will not come to any harm now I have removed the bone of contention.'

'I must make sure . . .'

'You are not going back there.' He drew into the curb and stopped the car. Seizing the strap of the seat belt, he pulled it round her with almost brutal force, drawing it tight. 'That one deserves no consideration for taking you to such a place. *Bon Sang*, when I think what might have happened to you!'

He started the car again and drove on.

'It wasn't his fault.' Jo loosened the belt which felt as though it were cutting her in two. 'I persuaded him to take me, so it isn't fair to blame him.'

'The eternal Eve,' Marcel mocked. 'He was weak like Adam.'

'He isn't weak!' Jo felt loyalty demanded that she

must defend her friend, though she was disappointed by his behaviour. 'He just hates refusing me anything.'

'And are you equally accommodating?'

For a second she did not grasp his meaning, then she flushed angrily. 'There's nothing like that between us.'

'*Tiens*, but you astonish me.'

'Of course you would think the worst,' Jo said loftily. 'We're just pals, but I suppose that would be beyond your understanding, being French.'

'Frenchmen and Englishmen are both equally human,' Marcel remarked drily. 'But I was forgetting, you are still a little girl.'

A remark which infuriated her. 'That young man thought I was grown up.'

'You would have been when he had finished with you,' Marcel said quietly. 'A most painful initiation.'

Jo shuddered. 'He wouldn't . . . I suppose he would.' She rubbed her neck where the belt had chafed her. 'But did *you* have to be so brutal?'

'A little brutality might bring you to your senses. You might have killed yourself if you had opened that door.'

She ought to be grateful to him, but his attitude froze her thanks; he so obviously thought she was a silly idiot who richly deserved the spanking he had once threatened her with.

'How did you know where I was?' she asked curiously.

'Jessica told us, she was worried about you knowing the reputation that place has got. Were you quite crazy to go there?'

She was thinking she had been just that, but she was not going to admit it to him.

'I wanted to see what it was like, and where I go is none of your business.'

'You would prefer I left you to that swine's tender mercies? You seemed pleased enough to see me when I appeared.'

'Oh, I was,' honesty compelled her to exclaim. 'But why did *you* come? I'd have thought Dad . . .'

'He is considerably older than I am,' Marcel cut in. 'I consider I am better equipped to deal with that sort of situation. My reactions are quicker. He might have got hurt.'

'So he might.' Jo shivered, recalling the knife. 'I . . . I'm very grateful to you, Mr de Savigny, for your timely rescue act, it was quite heroic.'

For the life of her she could not keep the note of sarcasm out of her voice. If only it had been anyone but Marcel who had saved her! It galled her that he had found her in such a predicament, and she hated being beholden to him. She glanced sideways at his profile beside her. She sensed he was very angry, and he drove fast with a fierce concentration as if working off on the car the fury he would like to wreak upon her, and he made no rejoinder to her crack about heroism. Feeling a little ashamed of herself, she said meekly:

'I promise I won't ever go there again.'

'You won't have the opportunity to do so.'

'How do you know?' she flashed. 'You'll be going back to France.'

'That is correct.'

Something in his tone caused her to throw him an uneasy glance, it seemed to conceal a menace. He slowed down, and when they reached a lay-by, he brought the car to a halt. He turned in his seat to face her, seemingly very big and forceful, so that Jo cowered back in against the upholstery.

'This last escapade of yours has exhausted your father's patience,' he told her coldly. 'He considers he has been too lenient with you and it is time you were restrained.'

'I don't believe it,' Jo cried indignantly. 'Daddy understands me. You've been getting at him because I hit you, and I suppose you told him about that.'

There was a bright moon and in the white light seeping through the windscreen the fading bruise on his face was clearly visible.

'I did not mention it,' Marcel said, 'I am no telltale. We agreed that this Terry Robinson is a bad influence and you should be removed from it.'

'Indeed?' Jo opened her eyes very wide. 'And how do you propose that that should be done?'

'It is quite simple. We have arranged that you shall accompany me back to France.'

Jo gaped at him incredulously, while from a nearby tree came the screech of a little owl, a sinister sound in the silence of the night.

CHAPTER FOUR

Jess had told Jo that Marcel was arranging with their father to take one of the sisters to his château with him for a visit, and both had been certain that it was Alison he had in mind. She was the eldest, the most sophisticated and the Frenchman had obviously been impressed by her. That either of the younger ones could be considered had never occurred to them, and certainly not to Jo, who thought he positively disliked her and had done her best to foster that dislike.

As she stared in dismay at the inscrutable face beside her, it flashed into her mind that Marcel had used her father's anger with her to offer this solution for her future with the sole purpose of effecting the retaliation he had promised her when she had struck his face. In his own home she would be entirely at his mercy, and her overwrought nerves conjured up pictures of the indignities, both physical and mental, that he would be in a position to inflict upon her.

'I won't go,' she cried stormily. 'You can't make me go, I'm over eighteen.'

'I have no intention of making you do anything,' he returned calmly. 'I appeal to your good sense. A sojourn abroad would be of great advantage to you.'

'I don't see how.'

'Perhaps you will, when you have considered the matter.'

'No need to do that. I would hate to leave my home, and . . . and Terry.'

'I fancy tonight's debacle will have lessened his attraction for you,' Marcel said drily, 'but was not his motorcycle the magnet?'

'It wasn't only that,' she declared hotly. 'I ... I'm fond of Terry.'

'Peculiar taste you have.'

If she were honest, Jo would have had to admit it was the pillion riding that had been her main reason for going out with Terry Robinson, and the youth himself had sunk in her estimation after his weak-kneed conduct at the Pelican. It was Marcel who had rescued her and his prompt action had aroused her unwilling admiration, but he had spoilt his gesture by making capital out of the unfortunate incident to gain her father's support for his own ends, and she said angrily:

'You think you've been very clever, don't you, but it won't work. When Daddy's had time to cool down, he'll have second thoughts about parting with me. He needs me to help with the horses. Jess can ride, but she's not keen; Alison has an allergy, she suffered from asthma when a child and the sweat and smell of horses brings it on—besides ...' She hesitated, on the verge of declaring that she was her father's favourite child, but though both he and she knew it, he tried to be strictly impartial and the fact was never acknowledged.

'I know all that,' Marcel told her, 'but your father is willing to do without your services for a while if it is for your good. I do not think he will change his mind. We had discussed it before this last escapade of yours, and he has always grieved that he could not afford to give you the same education that he gave your elder sister. A stay in France will enlarge your viewpoint and have cultural advantages for you.'

Jo drew away from him as far as the seat would allow and retorted bitingly:

'I don't think he'll care for the sort of education you

intend to give me, and when I've told him what you did in the forest, he won't consider you're a fit guardian for me.'

'Oh, that!' Marcel laughed merrily. 'That was only a game, a diversion to enliven a morning's *ennui*. Any man who has any red blood in him can be pardoned for kissing a pretty girl.' Jo flushed with annoyance. So that was all she had been, a passing amusement! Marcel went on:

'Kisses leave no mark, as a riding crop does.'

The bruise on his face was still discernible, proof of her violent action, and that, Jo knew, her father would not easily forgive. He would not believe that Marcel would go beyond kissing her, and quite possibly would think she had provoked him. His daughters had taught him to accept that such demonstrations were a feature of modern life.

'But you threatened reprisals,' she reminded him. 'Is this the start of them?'

'It is nothing of the sort. All I require is a companion for Thérèse, who has few friends of her own age since she left school. I need someone who can ride, as she is an accomplished horsewoman. As for anything else, . . .' he waved one slim hand, 'I spoke in jest. At the château the situation will be changed. You will be a guest, and my position there does not permit of such frivolities.'

Jo was further incensed to learn that what had been to her a traumatic experience was to him merely a joke. He had lifted his head proudly as he mentioned his position, and he looked every inch the lord of the manor, so that it was presumption to imagine he would condescend to amorous advances. As for the sister, she envisioned a haughty French aristocrat with Marcel's fine profile, who would be intimidating.

'Your sister must be much older than I,' she remarked, because she knew he was about ten years her senior. 'She'll find me too immature to be a friend.'

'Actually she is your age,' she was informed. 'There is a big gap between us. Let me tell you a little about her and then you will appreciate her position.'

'I'm not stopping you,' Jo returned ungraciously, as he glanced at her enquiringly. She already felt sure there could be no rapport between herself and Thérèse de Savigny.

'As my father held positions abroad and Maman would not leave Paris, my parents were often parted,' Marcel went on, his eyes fixed broodingly upon the landscape beyond the wind screen. 'Thérèse was the result of their last reunion. Maman was happy to have a girl, whom she could dress up as if she were a doll and indulge, and Thérèse was pert and amusing, but she tired of her as she grew older, and when Papa died she abandoned her to return to Paris, leaving her with Grand'mère as she had always left me, for whom she had little use. Eventually she too died, in her latest lover's arms.' Marcel's tone was bitter; evidently he resented his mother's neglect. 'Thérèse went to school, of course, but now she has left, she is always badgering me to let her live in Paris, but it is not suitable. She is too like her mother to be trusted on her own. I hope a young companion may be beneficial, so knowing our old friend Roger Thornton had three daughters, I came here to ... what do you say ... kill two birds with one stone, purchase a stallion, and obtain a friend for Thérèse.'

'Lucifer and me?' Jo thought he showed scant sympathy for his sister's point of view. Life in an old château with an ageing grandmother could not be very lively, she should be allowed to lead her own existence, train for a profession perhaps, but Marcel's ideas were old-fashioned. He was probably planning a marriage of convenience for her. She went on sweetly:

'Aren't you afraid I'll contaminate your sister with my reprehensible conduct?'

He smiled confidently. 'You have not gone so far that you cannot be reclaimed, and Thérèse is not a weak character. Besides, I shall be there to make sure you don't get into mischief.'

'Always assuming that I'll be coming.' The suggestion that she would be kept under his constant surveillance was galling.

'You will come,' he said with certainty.

'Not if I can help it. Why don't you take Alison? You get on with her, and she'd be amenable. She'd love to go.'

'I don't want to encourage expectations I can't fulfil,' Marcel said with a slight frown, thus betraying that he was aware of Alison's fancy for him and had no intention of becoming seriously involved. 'She can't ride, being allergic to horses,' he reminded her. 'I am very proud of my stables and the animals play a big part in our lives.'

In spite of herself, Jo's interest quickened.

'Do you race them?'

'Occasionally. I am hoping to breed a winner from Lucifer.'

'You mastered him all right,' Jo conceded, 'but I'm a different proposition.'

Marcel grinned wickedly. 'The same treatment might work with you.'

'The more you beat them, the better they be?'

'I think that saying does not mention a horse, and regarding women, I have never found it necessary to lift my hand to one . . . yet.'

There was an ominous glitter in his eyes, but it might have been a trick of the moonlight.

'There's always a first time,' Jo said audaciously.

'Exactly so.'

Jo's eyes dropped to his brown hands resting idly on the steering wheel, fine nervous hands, but strong and capable. He had more than once told her that she deserved a beating, but opportunities to incur his displeasure at the château would appear to be few. She reiterated firmly:

'I'm not coming.'

'You might be persuaded.' He looked at her significantly. 'You say you are fond of your *bien-aimé*. It would not be impossible to make out a case against him. He rides a motorcycle when under the influence of drink, and he enticed you into bad company.'

'I told you I made him take me, and he's not been caught by the police . . . Oh!' She put her hand to her mouth, realising she was giving Terry away.

'He will be if he attempts to ride home tonight.'

'So you've set a trap for him? How despicable! Don't you realise he may lose his licence?'

'That might be a good thing, since he is a public menace.'

'Are you quite unscrupulous when you want to get your own way?' Jo demanded indignantly.

'The end justifies the means,' he returned cryptically.

Jo did not want Terry to get into trouble, though she had no great wish to see him again, and she was a little puzzled by Marcel's insistence that she should go to France. He could not really care what she did or with whom she went. He must be motivated by consideration for her father, for whom he had a warm regard, and it must be Roger's decision that she should go. That wounded her, because though he deplored her madcap pranks, she would never have believed that he was prepared to banish her until Marcel told her so. If he continued to be obdurate, she was in no position to defy him, for she was dependent upon him financially and had small chance of being able to find a situation as a groom, the care of horses being her only asset, as the occupation was overstocked with eager aspirants prepared to work for a minimal wage.

Feeling herself abandoned, she saw the moonlit scene before her become misted with sudden tears, which she hastily wiped away with the back of her hand, hoping Marcel would not notice her weakness. She seldom cried, but the night's proceedings had proved too much for her, and that her predicament was her own fault was no consolation. She endeavoured to stifle a sob.

Marcel was too observant not to see her distress. He put his arm around her, drawing her close to his side, and handed her a clean handkerchief from his pocket. Forgetting who he was, aware only that he was offering sympathy, Jo buried her face in his shoulder and wept unrestrainedly. Gently he stroked her hair, then gathered her into his arms. As her tears abated, Jo wiped her eyes, and realised that it was not her father to whom she was clinging. His close hold was definitely not paternal, and a disturbance in her nerves caused her to tremble. She tried to draw away, but his arms tightened, and she had a strong impulse to put hers around his neck. Embrace Marcel? Preposterous notion! His face was only inches from her own, and he bent his head, lightly touching her lips with his. A thrill of excitement shot through her, and she relaxed against him, but he made no attempt to avail himself of her response. Instead he loosened his clasp and let her slip back into her seat.

Jo stared at him wide-eyed. Tenderness from Marcel, the tyrant, the aggressor, was the last thing that she had expected. That she had been affected by it was also inexplicable. He had turned away from her and was gazing out of the windscreen. His hands, back on the steering wheel, shook slightly, and a pulse beat in his cheek, but she failed to grasp the significance of these slight signs.

At length, when the silence began to be oppressive, he moved, reaching for his cheeroots.

'Better now?' he asked as he lit one, winding down the window to release the smoke.

'Oh, Marcel what must you think of me,' she burst out. 'I hardly ever cry, it was just . . . just . . . .'

'*Pauvre petite*, this evening's events have been too much for you,' he said kindly. 'And I quite enjoyed the role of comforter.'

She touched his shoulder. 'I . . . I've damped your jacket.'

'*N'importe*. I have often had to dry Thérèse's childish tears.'

'But I'm grown up,' Jo protested, knowing that the emotions he had stirred in her had not been those of a child. A thought occurred to her, an excuse to save her face. 'I . . . I drank too much at the Pelican, drink can make you maudlin, can't it?'

The corners of Marcel's mouth twitched.

'It has been known to do so,' he agreed gravely. Then he smiled. 'Come, Josephine, why are you making such a fuss about a visit to France? It will be a new experience for you, and I know you are adventurous. I have some superb horses for you to ride, and your family, and your *bien-aimé*, if you want him, will still be here when you return, if you return.' His smile widened. 'I can promise you better entertainment than the Pelican.'

'Well, perhaps I will come,' Jo acceded, beginning to think the visit might have something to recommend it. 'But why do you say *if* I return? You haven't got some scheme to marry me off to some buddie of yours, have you? I've no dowry worth mentioning.'

'I have no such thought, but you might fall in love ... with France.'

'That is most improbable.'

'All things are possible,' Marcel remarked sententiously.

'Just the same, I think Alison would be much more suitable, even though she doesn't ride.'

'There I disagree.'

'I suppose you think I'm safer,' Jo said scornfully. 'Since you regard me as a child.' She looked at him provocatively. 'Suppose I end by falling in love with you?'

A curious expression came into his eyes, he seemed about to say something, then checked himself. After a pause, he asked her:

'Is there any danger of that? You dislike me, don't you?'

'It often begins with a little aversion, doesn't it?' Jo enquired, her eyes sparkling with mischief.

'But I am a lot older than ... Terry, for example.'

'But you wanted a young wife to mould into the way you wanted her to be,' Jo reminded him, suddenly recalling a former conversation. 'But don't worry, I've no wish to be moulded into any shape but my own, so you're quite safe.'

'Don't be too sure of that,' he said in a changed voice. Then he laughed. 'You are a provocative little devil, Josephine. I shall tell your father to chastise you.'

'Unlike you, Daddy doesn't believe in corporal punishment, and I'm quite sure when he has thought things over he will change his mind.' Jo was unwilling to accept that her father could be persuaded to part with her. 'In which case of course I'll stay here.'

'This time, *ma chère*, you have gone too far,' Marcel told her with a return of his former severe manner. 'You will find him adamant.'

That Jo still could not credit; she was sure if she were really contrite he would relent. Marcel started up the car and they continued their journey through the black and white night. They passed stretches of heathland, crossed a molten silver stream with above them the wide expanse of the sky, where a few stars were bright enough to compete with the moon. Through the half open window Jo caught a familiar sound.

'Stop, Marcel, please stop.'

'What is it,' he asked, as drawing into the verge he killed the engine. 'Something wrong?'

'Listen.'

Clear and sweet a bird's song trilled from a clump of bushes.

'*Un rossignol*,' Marcel murmured.

'They are becoming rare. Oh, Marcel, I couldn't bear to leave all this!'

'The valley of the Loire is not without beauty,' Marcel remarked drily.

'Yes, but . . .' Her voice faded, and both fell silent as the nightingale's 'jug-jug' preluded another burst of melody. Marcel seemed as delighted by the feathered minstrel as Jo was, and for once they were in harmony, wrapped in the enchantment of the night. Wearied by the long day and its traumatic climax, Jo almost unconsciously leaned against her escort, as she would have done had he been her father or Terry, having released the catch of her seat belt. Tentatively Marcel put his arm round her, and as she made no protest, drew her close to his side, his hand resting lightly upon her breast. She forgot her animosity against him, finding his clasp oddly comforting, and as the pressure of his hand increased, the resulting stir in her blood was pleasurable. The bird's song suddenly ceased, and she murmured a faint protest as Marcel withdrew his arm.

'It must be late and your father will be anxious,' he said prosaically, as he started the engine. 'We must get on.'

Jo flushed as she realised how closely they had been entwined. Their mutual enjoyment no longer seemed an adequate excuse for such familiarity.

'Were you trying to flirt with me, Mr de Savigny?' she asked cheekily.

'I was not flirting, Josephine,' he retorted. 'Merely providing a support which you seemed to need.' He shot her a sly glance. 'But I am glad my touch does not repel you.'

'Should it?' she enquired innocently. 'I'd forgotten you weren't my father.'

'I'm hardly old enough to be that.' Marcel sounded annoyed.

'Not unless you were extraordinarily precocious,' Jo said provocatively.

'That sort of remark deserves a demonstration you would dislike,' Marcel told her. 'For both our sakes, you had better guard your tongue. Any further marks upon my face might invite awkward questions.'

Jo felt a thrill of excitement. If Marcel kissed her again, really kissed her as he had done in the forest, would she object? She was shocked to discover that she wanted him to do so. It must be the drink, she decided, which could arouse amorous feelings as well as maudlin ones. She must be careful when she arrived in France. Didn't they drink a lot of wine, which she was unused to? Arrived in France! She was not going. She would persuade her father to let her stay at home, and Roger never resisted her pleas for long.

But as Marcel had warned her, Roger Thornton was adamant. He had decided that the liberty she had enjoyed was too dangerous for a young woman of her temperament. Jo had never before known him to be so stern. Terry Robinson, he declared, was a menace, and she must be put beyond reach of his corrupting influence. When out of loyalty she tried to defend him, Roger shouted her down. Didn't she know that half the Pelican clientele was on drugs, and probably Terry was too?

'I'm sure he's not,' Jo cried vehemently.

'How do you know?' her father countered. 'And you're just the sort of idiot who would try them for kicks, and before you knew where you were you'd be addicted. If you think so much of that wretched youth, you'll go without any more fuss. Otherwise I'll tell old Robinson what his boy's been up to, and withdraw my custom from his garage.'

Jo had a shrewd idea that at least half his delinquencies were unknown to Terry's father, and the garage serviced all Roger's vehicles, including the farm machinery. So she was able to pose as the self-sacrificing heroine who submitted to tyranny for her lover's sake. Only Terry was not her lover and never likely to

be, and she doubted if he would appreciate her sacrifice, or even realise that it was one. But it was a face-
saver when she had to admit to Marcel that she had
capitulated.

'I don't want to get dear Terry into trouble,' she told
him.

'That, *my petite*, is beyond your power to prevent,'
was his retort.

Jo feared he was right, and said no more. She was
overwhelmed by the change in her hitherto indulgent
father, and had no fight left in her. She was no longer
sure that she wanted to stay at the farm since both he
and Terry had failed her.

Disappointed that Jo was to go and not herself,
Alison became spiteful.

'It is to be hoped you'll learn some decent manners
among civilised people,' she told Jo crushingly. 'At least
you'll have to take care of your appearance and eat at
the table. I'm afraid Marcel doesn't realise what a little
savage you are, and his good intentions will be wasted
upon you.'

'Perhaps his intentions aren't as good as you think,'
Jo returned, goaded beyond endurance, and forgetting
to be discreet.

Alison looked her up and down contemptuously. Jo
had just come in from the stables and her jeans and
shirt were decorated with hayseeds, her hair in wild disorder.

'Good Lord, he can't feel anything but revulsion
when you look as you do now! Anyway, a chit like you
can have no appeal for a man of the world like him.'

'Well, you don't seem to have made a hit with him,
since he's leaving you behind,' Jo retaliated.

Alison winced and sighed. 'Of course I knew he
wasn't serious.'

'Monsieur de Savigny is the love 'em and leave 'em type,' Jo declared, feeling a little sorry for her sister. 'Believe me, Ally, I'd much rather you were going.'

She realised with surprise that that was not quite true. She had become reconciled to visiting the château and was intrigued by its master.

'You're being sent away because you're in disgrace,' Alison snapped. 'And I hope Marcel takes a strap to you if you don't behave!'

A remark that revived some of Jo's former fears. Was Marcel going to try to discipline her with her father's consent? Then she recalled his gentleness when she had wept. He had treated her like an unhappy child, but he had shown he was capable of kindness. She did not believe he would bully her.

Her father went up to London to obtain her passport, so there would be no delay on that account. Her mother fussed over her clothes. She must have some dresses besides her usual trousers and tops, and a proper riding outfit.

'Unnecessary expense,' Jo objected.

'No daughter of mine goes to stay with aristocrats looking like a tramp,' Annette declared.

The 'aristocrats' stuck in Jo's throat.

'Oh, Jess, what have I let myself in for?' she wailed to her younger sister. 'If they're stuck up and starchy I won't be able to bear it.'

Jess was unsympathetic. 'You don't know your luck. Wish I was going. To stay at a genuine château under Marcel's wing! It would be heaven.'

'That's no inducement,' Jo retorted. 'You've got a crush on him, but I haven't. I only hope it won't be hell.'

She was dragged off unwillingly to Ipswich to have her wardrobe replenished. She hated trying on clothes. The saleswomen were in raptures over her tall, slim figure, which was the sort for which most of their dresses were designed. Jo's taste when she could be made to state a preference was for plainly cut garments, but Annette thought a young girl should be decked in frills and flounces, preferably in white.

'I will not look like a wedding cake,' Jo said firmly, stepping out of a nylon dress with a net overlay. 'If I must have an evening dress, I'll take the black.'

Which was not a bad choice, for black showed up the whiteness of those parts of her arms and neck not usually exposed and enhanced her burnished hair. The dress in question was of polyester and designed on simple, flowing lines, the high waist bound in with a sash of silver brocade.

'Too old for you,' Annette insisted.

'I want to look old,' Jo returned. 'I'm not a school-girl.'

She wanted Marcel to realise she was an adult, and after some further argument, her mother gave in. The new jodhpurs pleased her, but she refused to have a hacking jacket. Shirts or sweaters would suffice. Over her travelling outfit, Annette had her way. Jo wanted a trouser suit, her mother a skirt. In the end they compromised, with a russet outfit, with a lemon blouse, natty waistcoat and a neat jacket.

'No hat,' Jo insisted. 'That I do bar.'

Throughout those final days Marcel had held aloof, confident that she would be unable to back out. Regarding her clothes, he suggested waiting until she arrived in Paris where they could break their journey and he would supervise her choice. That idea Jo firmly vetoed. Shopping with her mother was bad enough, but with Marcel it would be infinitely worse. Roger, who was present, raised his brows enquiringly.

'What do you know about women's gear, my boy?'

'I have a grandmother, and a young sister, also lady friends who all applaud my taste.'

'That's cissy,' Jo said bluntly.

'The best couturiers are men,' Marcel observed mildly. 'When I was a boy, my mother took me to view several collections, and young as I was, I knew what would suit her.'

'Of course you're French,' Jo amended hastily, seeing her father frown at her implied criticism. She looked at Marcel speculatively, thinking that at his age he probably had had a succession of mistresses and bought their clothes. With the naïveté of innocence she exaggerated the possibility. Perhaps it was as well Alison was not going to France. She might end up as one of his *bien-aimées*, but he presented no temptation to her, and it had been dinned into her that she could be none to him. His reasons for taking her were bona fide.

She caught his quizzical glance and had a suspicion that he guessed her thoughts, which caused her to blush fierily.

'After all, it is I who have to look at what my female connections wear,' he drawled. 'And it pains me when they make guys of themselves.'

Jo was thankful that she had resisted the wedding cake, which she was sure he would consider poor taste, and wondered if he would like the black. Then she tossed her bright head defiantly. His likes and dislikes were nothing to her.

He was watching her, as he often did, with a little enigmatic smile on his thin lips. Even when he was apparently deep in conversation with someone else she found his eyes upon her. At times she experienced a moment of panic. The de Savignys might be old family friends and her father trusted Marcel implicitly, but in his own home he would be absolute master and she would have to submit to his whims. She would have no friend or ally at the château, for naturally his grandmother and sister would side with him. Would they, as Ally insisted, find her uncouth? She felt she needed reassurance upon that point.

As she never saw him alone, she waylaid him one morning when he brought Lucifer back from exercise. The stallion was to be despatched by sea, while they followed by air, and one of Marcel's grooms had come over especially to take charge of the animal. The man came forward to take the horse to his box as Jo crossed the yard.

'I know all the arrangements have been made,' she said hurriedly, with her eyes on the retreating man and horse, noting mechanically that the groom seemed to have won Lucifer's confidence. 'But it's not too late to change your mind. My sister says you don't realise what a little savage I am, and there's no hope of improving me, if that's your idea. For your sister's sake, hadn't you better reconsider?'

He regarded her through half-closed lids, a sleepy sensual look which caused her nerves to quiver.

'I know exactly what you are, Josephine, so what your sister says will not influence me. I have no wish to improve you, you are refreshingly natural, though it might become you to acquire a little polish.'

Her grey eyes fell beneath his close regard. She was never sure when he was mocking or serious.

'I don't want to be . . . er . . . polished,' she said rebelliously.

'You are being childish, Josephine. The process will not be painful and will fit you for the position you will one day fill.'

'As Daddy's right-hand man? That doesn't need polish.'

He made an impatient gesture with one hand.

'You are not a man, Josephine, and a woman should be cognisant of the social graces. Life at the château will help you to attain them.'

Jo opened her eyes very wide. 'I thought I was going to be your sister's English teacher-cum-companion. She may need the—what was it?—social graces, but I won't.'

'Do you always want to be a little savage?' he asked.

'That's Ally's opinion of me, not mine.' Her glance strayed to the faint discoloration which was all that was left of the mark on his face. 'Will you ever forget or forgive that blow I gave you?'

'I was not thinking of that,' he told her. 'But now you mention it, I have not given up hope that you will one day make amends for it. I believe you have repented it ever since.'

She had more than once, but his superior tone made her bristle, though she would never admit it.

'I acted according to my savage nature,' she returned. 'If provoked, I might do it again.'

'I don't think you would. Your heart would not be in it.'

Startled, she exclaimed: 'What do you know about my heart?'

'More than you do, but realisation will come to you when you have got over this tiresome adolescent stage.'

Jo wriggled her shoulders under her sweater.

'More conundrums,' she complained. 'I wish you'd speak plain English, Marcel.'

'But I am not English, and when the time comes I will explain . . . in French. And that is something you will have a chance to learn. You don't know my language, do you?'

'Doesn't your family speak English?' she asked, alarmed.

'Perfectly, they are well educated,' he returned. 'Several languages is considered essential to be that.'

Jo sighed.

'So I'm ignorant as well as uncivilised. You'd much better leave me behind, Marcel.'

But even as she suggested it, she felt a sudden qualm. Could it be that she was afraid he would take her at her word? Wasn't that what she wanted? She simply did not understand herself.

Marcel shook his head, smiling.

'Not on your life, *ma petite sauvage*. But this I can promise you. When you return . . . if you return . . . you will be tamed.'

With that he turned on his heel and strode away, leaving her staring after him wondering if he had uttered a threat or had spoken in jest.

CHAPTER FIVE

Jo arrived in France on a day of sunshine and showers with big white clouds billowing across the summer blue. She was excited by the novelty of flying and the prospect of viewing the French capital, though their sojourn would be brief. They left England very early in the morning so that Marcel could show her some of the sights before the long drive down to the Loire. His car was parked at the airport awaiting his return. In England he had used one of her father's, when he needed one. On the night before, Roger had taken leave of her in private, admonishing her to make herself pleasant to her hosts.

'The old lady is a bit formidable,' he had warned her, 'but she has a heart of gold. I met her some time back, and she's had a lot of trouble, losing her only son and her daughter-in-law having no use for her. Marcel is a good man in spite of his French manners. If I have to lose you I'd rather it was to him than someone like young Terry, which is all you'll meet round here.'

'But you're not losing me,' she had cried, a little puzzled by his words. 'I'll be coming back and everything will be as it was before.'

He had shaken his head sadly as he said: 'Nothing ever is. You'll be changed.'

'Not if I know it,' she had insisted stoutly.

Roger drove them to the airport, and the family assembled in various stages of undress to see them off.

Annette, who was secretly relieved she was not to be parted from Alison, who was her favourite, besought Jo to make the most of her opportunities, Jess was tearful, while Alison strove to conceal her envy as she wished Jo well. Roger dropped them at reception, saying he had to get back, and his final farewell was almost perfunctory under Marcel's quizzical gaze. After he had disappeared, Jo wiped a tear from her eye, while her love of adventure reasserted itself. She was wearing her new outfit, and Marcel eyed her appreciatively while their luggage was being weighed.

'It seems the taming process has already begun,' he remarked.

'Don't kid yourself,' she had retorted. 'I'm only temporarily disguised.'

He had guided her through the intricacies of passport control and boarding the plane, amused by her eager curiosity and her naïve criticisms of her fellow passengers. She looked younger than her nineteen years with her face flushed by excitement and her eyes bright with interest.

From the airport, Marcel drove into Paris and took her up to Montmartre for lunch in the open-air café beside the meringue-shaped cupolas of the Sacré Cœur, with a wide view of the city spread before them. Since he had arrived on his native soil, he seemed much more foreign to her. Sitting opposite to her under a coloured umbrella that shaded them from the sun, his fine features, smooth olive skin, inky brows and lashes were conspicuous among the crowd surrounding them, nearly all of whom had blunt Anglo-Saxon faces, being mostly British or American tourists.

For the first time she fully appreciated his distinguished looks, which together with his imperious manner obtained for him prompt service. Not that he was in the least discourteous, it was simply those who served him recognised his quality and were hopeful of lavish *pourboires*. Towards herself, he was kindly indulgent. She might have been a favourite niece he was treating, but he was not old enough to be her uncle and she began to resent his attitude. He chose the food and the wine, saying she would enjoy this or that without consulting her, and discoursed impersonally about the history of the city. When they reached the dessert, she was served with a concoction of fruit, meringue and whipped cream, which would have delighted a child, and she said reproachfully:

'You're always accusing me of being immature, but you're acting as if I hadn't a mind of my own.'

He regarded her lazily, his eyes very blue in his brown face.

'In what way have I erred?'

'This.' She indicated the sweet. 'It's delicious, of course, but terribly fattening.'

'You could do with a few more curves,' he observed, studying her critically. 'And you would have been lost with the French menu. I will remember in future that you prefer bread and cheese.'

Which was what he was eating himself. Jo would much rather have the sweet, but said nothing.

'I don't suppose we'll have any meals out together after we've arrived?' she enquired wistfully. Surprisingly she was enjoying their lunch together and his company. Being the sole object of his attention made her feel important, and she noticed every female within range looked at Marcel with interest.

'Unlikely,' he confirmed.

'Your sister doesn't eat out?'

'Upon occasion. We do most of our entertaining in restaurants instead of our own homes, but then we will dine and lunch *en famille*, not tête-à-tête.'

When she would be a mere appendage and beneath his notice.

'We do, however, invite guests to the château upon special occasions,' he went on. 'I believe Grand'mère is planning a *bal masqué* for Thérèse's *anniversaire*, which you call birthday. That is next month and you will be here for it.'

'That will be lovely,' Jo said flatly. *Bal masqué* sounded dreadfully formal and old-fashioned. They might even dance quadrilles, a far cry from the pop music and modern gyrations which she enjoyed.

'When is your birthday?' Marcel enquired.

'Next month too.'

'*Alors*, you can celebrate together.'

'I'm sure Thérèse won't want me butting in to steal her thunder,' Jo told him morosely. 'It's her special day.'

'She is not so petty, but she may insist that a double occasion necessitates double expenditure.' He smiled ruefully. 'You and she will have fun devising your costumes, for of course it will be fancy dress.'

'I shall come as a tramp,' Jo decided, thinking of the expense of a period costume. Her father paid her a quarterly allowance instead of a salary and she did not intend to waste it upon elaborate garments for a party that did not appeal to her and would probably be very uncomfortable.

'That I shall not allow. You must appear as a lady of quality,'

Jo laughed. 'I don't see me being that, it wouldn't suit me at all.'

'We will see,' Marcel decreed with an ominous glint in his eyes, which foretold that he meant to have his way.

'Yes, we will, won't we,' Jo agreed sweetly, determined to thwart him. Thérèse would be a possible ally, not wanting to have a rival at her own party. That started another train of thought.

'Is she pretty?' she asked.

'Who? Oh, Thérèse. Moderately,' he told her with brotherly candour. 'She has the de Savigny nose.' He stroked his own handsome organ. 'It is rather too much in a girl's face.'

'It suits yours,' Jo told him candidly, admiring its aquiline shape. 'Mine's a snub.'

'I find it quite charming,' Marcel declared gallantly, and Jo frowned.

'I wasn't fishing for compliments.'

'That is something you must learn—to accept them gracefully.'

'Oh, I see, you're testing me and I fell at the first fence. None of my acquaintances bother to pay them.'

Terry certainly had not. He took her appearance for granted.

'How remiss! But what else can one expect from clodhoppers?' Marcel exclaimed scornfully. He went on solemnly, but with a twinkle in his eyes, 'We will try again. That suit you are wearing is very becoming and you look like a dewy rose.'

Which was not so far-fetched as it sounded, for Jo's cheeks were delicately tinted and looked as if they might be soft as a petal. But Jo was incensed.

'Draw it mild, Marcel, I really can't cope with that sort of rubbish. It makes me laugh!'

Marcel sighed in mock despair.

'I only hope my countrymen find you original.'

'Is it original not to appreciate insincerity?'

'But they may be sincere.' He leaned forward and lightly stroked her cheek with two fingers. 'Your skin is soft as a rose leaf.'

'Please don't.' His action had set her nerves quivering. She went on with heightened colour, 'Ally gave me some special cream which she said would prevent my skin from becoming leathery from exposure. Evidently it worked.'

Marcel laughed. 'You should not betray your trade secrets, though your frankness is amusing.'

'I'm glad you find it so,' she returned tartly. Her expression became anxious. 'Will there be many young men at this dance?' She did not feel equal to dealing with sophisticated Frenchmen.

'All the countryside will come to honour Thérèse.'

'Then please forget it's my birthday too. I wish I hadn't told you.'

'Impossible. I will not defraud you of your dues.'

'But I'm only going to be your sister's companion and haven't got any dues, as you put it. I should be in the background, if I appear at all.'

'Of course you will appear, and you will not skulk in the background.' He threw up his head haughtily with what she was beginning to term his Monsieur le Comte air. 'I promised your father you would be treated as one of the family. How then can we ignore your special day?' His eyes narrowed and he looked at her keenly. 'I have a reason for wishing you to shine upon that day.'

Something in his regard caused her to feel uneasy, and she said crossly:

'You'll be disappointed. I shan't have had time to

acquire those social graces you're so keen on.'

'You will learn fast. Coffee?' He beckoned to a waiter.

'Yes, please. I'm only a gauche country girl, Marcel.'

He ordered the coffee, then turned to her.

'Just be your natural self, Josephine, and all will be well.'

'I'm always that,' Jo sighed. 'I expect the girls you usually associate with are much more sophisticated.'

'One can weary of sophistication. I appreciate your complete naturalness.'

Jo sighed again. 'What you really mean is you find my blunders funny.'

The waiter brought the coffee with also a cognac for Marcel. It was white, in wine glasses, with half an inch of cream on top. Jo had never seen coffee served so, but said nothing, fearing to appear ignorant. Marcel told her:

'You have not committed any solecisms yet.'

'Having been here only half a day, but just you wait.' She took a sip of the coffee, smiling mischievously at him over the brim of her glass. They had drunk wine with their excellent meal, and she felt her spirits rise. Marcel seemed to find her entertaining, and he was planning a dance for her in conjunction with his sister, so he could not dislike her after all, and perhaps the *bal masqué* would be fun.

A woman at the next table stood up preparatory to departure. She was one of the very few Parisians present, and her whole appearance, from her chic little toque to her high-heeled shoes, was stylish perfection. Jo saw Marcel turn his head to look at her with obvious admiration, and the woman threw him a sly glance. Then her escort, a prosperous-looking German, hurried her away, while Marcel's eyes followed her retreat. He seemed to have forgotten Jo in some sensual fantasy of his own evoked by the Frenchwoman. Jo drained her glass feeling deflated, realising anew her own shortcomings. She could not compare with that smart Parisian whose wit doubtless matched her appearance. Despite her nineteen years, she was only a raw adolescent to whom Marcel was being kind. The absent look he gave her was almost condescending. Determined to shake his complacency, she said abruptly:

'How many mistresses have you had, Marcel?'

In that he looked startled, she achieved her object, then his eyes crinkled with amusement, but he spoke severely:

'That question, *enfant du diable*, is an impertinence.'

'Is it?' Her wide grey eyes showed only innocent curiosity. 'You told me to be my natural self, and I've wondered. You aren't married and you're French, so you must have at least one. Don't try to kid me there aren't any women in your life.'

For some reason which she could not analyse she was eager to know if he were involved and with whom.

He said repressively: 'If there are, that is my affair.'

'Of course, but don't men like to boast of their conquests? Tell me about her, I won't split. I imagine she's small, dark and dainty, very vivacious and very, very chic. You go to her when you want relaxation from the cares of running your estate and your grandmother and sister are being tiresome.'

Deliberately she had described someone the antithesis of herself and she watched him covertly for his reaction, but Marcel's face was inscrutable, a little sardonic smile playing about his mouth. As he made no comment, she demanded impatiently:

'Am I right?'

'Your perspicacity is amazing,' he returned coolly.
'You have drawn a striking picture of her, especially the
very, very chic. But this is not a subject for polite conversation.'

Her impertinence had been rewarded by apparent
confirmation, and Jo felt a pang of . . . could it be jealousy? Hastily she assured herself that Marcel's love
affairs did not concern her, but his involvement explained why he had chosen her instead of Alison, whose
good looks and obvious fancy for him might offend his
lady. No one could fear rivalry from her ingenuous self,
and she had no desire whatever for amorous attentions
from him. His reasons for bringing her to the château
were genuine, and once she was introduced to Thérèse
he would ignore her as long as she behaved herself.
Why did the prospect seem so bleak? Marcel's amusement increased as he noticed her ill-concealed dejection.
It seemed to afford him considerable satisfaction.

'Have you finished?' he asked. 'We have not much
time to spare and I want to show you the Champs
Elysées and the Arc de Triomphe before we leave.'

Jo's mercurial spirits began to rise.

'And Notre Dame and the Latin Quarter?'

'Another time, they are not on our route.'

'But you said there wouldn't be another time.'

'I daresay I could arrange for you to have a few days
here with Thérèse, and she will show you round.'

The prospect left her cold. The visit would lose its
charm without Marcel's company.

'That would be very nice,' she said primly, keeping
her eyes lowered.

Again satisfaction showed in his expression.

'You are very transparent,' he observed.

'I haven't got anything to hide,' she retorted. 'Not like you and your murky affairs.'

He frowned. "All the same, it would be wise not to boast of your adventures at the Pelican to Thérèse.'

It was tit for tat, and Jo flushed.

'I shouldn't dream of doing so,' she said stiffly. 'Boast is the wrong word. I . . . I know I was very foolish to go there.'

She hoped the admission would please him, but he was regarding her sternly.

'Worse than that. If I had been your father I would have whipped you.'

'I would have preferred that to being exiled to France, and Daddy would never lay a finger on a woman.'

'You surprise me. However were you conceived?'

'Oh, don't be so absurd!' Jo laughed, blushed and then sobered as she recalled what Marcel had done to her when he had decided she was too old to be spanked. He told her:

'I am sorry you regard this visit as a banishment, Josephine. I thought you were enjoying it.'

'Oh, this part's super,' she exclaimed childishly. 'But I haven't met your people yet.' Apprehension showed in her eyes.

'Do not be alarmed. They cannot eat you.'

'But you want them to polish me, which is worse.'

'Now you are being absurd,' Marcel laughed. 'Come along, we must be on our way.'

By devious routes he drove her down to the Place de la Concorde, which was too thronged with traffic to allow her more than a glimpse of it. She admired Marcel's skill in dealing with the mass of vehicles. He was as competent with a car as he was with a horse, so

perhaps his arrogance was excusable; she had never yet
seen him at a loss.

The broad expanse of the Champs Elysées, lined with
shops, cafés and show-rooms, seemed to her to exude
vitality and gaiety, and she wished they had time to
linger, and when they reached the Arc de Triomphe, she
recognised it from the pictures she had seen of it. All
too soon thèy had left the heart of the city behind them
and were traversing suburbs, ugly tenements and the
factories that encircle the capital. They were heading
south, and with every kilometre Jo's spirits sank lower.
What sort of reception would the de Savignys give her?

Marcel took the Nationale 20 and town gave place to
country. The road took them over the plateau of the
Beauce, vast acres of wheat turning to gold. It was not
at all interesting, nor was Marcel's conversation. He
was telling her that several millions of years ago, a tilt
in the earth had caused the river Loire to alter course
from north to west, and a much inferior stream now
filled its old bed. The river curved sharply to the left, to
finally emerge at Nantes in South Brittany. It was along
its middle stretch that most of the famous châteaux
stood. Replete with good food and feeling sleepy, Jo
heard his pleasant voice without taking in much of what
he said. From geography he went on to history.
Orléans, which they would pass, had been relieved by
Jeanne d'Arc at the start of her campaign, defeating the
English army that laid siege to it. That had been the
beginning of the end of English dominance in France.
Anjou in the basin of the Loire was the homeland of
that great King and bad husband and father, Henry II,
son of the Geoffroi who took the *planta genista* to be
his badge, from which his descendants became known
as Plantagenets. Henry had died in Chinon, on the

banks of the river, and he, his wife, Eleanor and his son, Richard Coeur de Lion, had been buried at nearby Fontevrault Abbey.

'So you might say there is one spot in Anjou that is forever England,' Marcel concluded his discourse.

'I suppose so,' Jo agreed, stifling a yawn. Such subjects were safer than more personal ones, and this was not the sort of education he had threatened her with in England, but that was to be forgotten now he had become the *grand seigneur*. She glanced a little wistfully at his fine profile; she had learned he had more alluring distractions in Paris, and he would not bore his *bien-aimée* with history.

From the Beauce they passed through the Forêt d'Orléans, a long narrow belt of forest where once the nobility of France had done their hunting. There were other forests in the vicinity, and the châteaux were in reality glorified hunting lodges; the chase had been the main recreation of those days.

Orléans was originally a Roman town, and in mediaeval times had rivalled Paris in importance. Now it was a much smaller city than Tours and Angers farther along the Loire. It still possessed its ancient walls, though, as elsewhere, more modern buildings had sprung up outside them. Within the walls are a number of Renaissance houses, in one of which the Dauphin Francis, husband of Mary Queen of Scots, had died. There was a huge Gothic cathedral, but Marcel said they had no time for sightseeing, Jo must come another day. He did drive into the town, and stopped in the square at the top of the Rue Royale, which led down to the bridge over the Loire. In it was an equestrian statue of Jeanne d'Arc, and Jo roused herself to admire it, for Joan of Arc had always been one of her heroines.

'Like you, she aped a man,' Marcel remarked. 'But it must have been necessary in her position.'

Jo's eyes shone. 'It must have been a great life, leading armies into battle.'

'And being burned at the stake?'

'She was betrayed,' Jo cried angrily. 'By men, of course. What brutes your sex can be!'

Marcel laughed and drove on. From Orléans river and road turned westward, running through water meadows and the vineyards had appeared. Five miles short of Blois, its great château visible on its little range of hills, Marcel turned north, through a picturesque market town, and then up a private road. They came to an imposing entry, its gates set ajar, beyond which an avenue of poplars led to a building at its far end.

'We have arrived—that is the Château de Savigny, my ancestral home,' Marcel told her as they drove down it. His tone was dry.

The long drive was straight as a ruler, and as they approached it, the château seemed to grow bigger and bigger, its windows lit by the rays of the sinking sun seemed to glow with inner light. There was a fine white façade, the original windows enlarged to tall narrow ones; at either end was a circular tower with a conical pepperpot roof. The trees ended, and there were smooth shaven lawns, ending in a paved courtyard in front of it. There were trees behind it, and outbuildings to one side, masked by shrubs.

Jo rubbed her eyes. It looked like something out of a fairy tale, she had not expected it to be so big, and she asked Marcel with awe:

'Does all that belong to you?'

'Unfortunately yes. I had far rather live on one of the farms, for that pile is very expensive to maintain. Eventually it will have to become a hotel or a museum like most of the others. I want to keep it as it is while my grandmother is alive. She has always lived here and it would break her heart to have to leave it. As châteaux go it is not very large, but for only the three of us . . .' He gave a Gallic shrug.

Jo sensed his devotion to the old lady who had reared him. As he slowed down, she said faintly:

'I can't imagine living in such a place.'

'That is what you are going to do, but never fear, familiarity is said to breed contempt, and you will soon become used to it.'

Jo could not believe she would ever feel contempt for the Château de Savigny. It was much too impressive.

He killed the engine and sat looking at his domain half ruefully, half affectionately. The entrance was imposing, a massive oak-studded door above a shallow flight of steps.

'We only use the front part,' he told her, 'and that is too large. The towers and the back parts are shut up.'

'Are they haunted?' Jo shivered slightly; the thought of numbers of empty rooms was eerie.

'I have never heard so.'

There had been no sign of life, but now the front door slowly opened, and a stately old man in some sort of livery came down the steps. He was followed by a young one, who wore a baize apron, who had come to take in their luggage. His elder was much too superior to handle suitcases.

The old man opened the car door, and addressed Marcel deferentially as Monsieur le Comte.

Monsieur le Comte looked at Jo ruefully.

'They will do it, tradition dies hard. No good telling them, the old ones anyway, that the title is obsolete.'

But to Jo he had become very much Monsieur le Comte, a being as proud and aloof as his own house, though 'house' was too homely a word to describe that vast pile. Gone was the entertaining companion of her journey, the guest at Greyfriars whom she had resented . . . and struck! However had she had the temerity to do it?

'*Madame est au salon,*' the old man told him.

'*Merci*, Gaston.'

Marcel sprang out of the car, came round to her side, opened the door, and unceremoniously bundled her out.

'Wake up, Josephine, my grandmother is waiting to be introduced.'

Jo stood blinking dazedly beside the car. Madame was waiting in the *salon*, was she? She was not human enough to come to the door to greet them. She thought how her own family would have come rushing out to welcome them. Good God, what had she got herself into? Marcel took her arm and conducted her to the door. It gave access to a vast hall with a fine oak staircase facing it, and a gallery running round it at first floor level. It reached the full height of the house and was lit by a glass dome in the roof which must be a modern innovation. A vast stone fireplace filled one wall, piled with great logs, which would be cheerful in winter but was depressing with the fire unlit. There were numerous doors, and Marcel led her through one of them into the *salon*. The room was huge, like the drawing-rooms in the stately homes Jo had occasionally visited. Four long windows were in the outer wall, a white marble fireplace with an ornate overmantel was opposite to them. The miscellaneous furniture was of different periods, and dim canvases in heavy gilt frames hung on the walls. Jo was relieved to notice there were electric light fittings; so the place did have some modern amenities.

She only gained a momentary impression of the room, for her attention was drawn to the woman regally seated on a velvet-covered chair by the window. Solange de Savigny was a replica of her ancestors; even her dress had a period look. It was long and full, made of some dark material with a cream lace bertha and elbow cuffs. Her snow-white hair was dressed high, and might have been powdered. She wore black net mittens, and jewels at her throat and in her ears. She can't be real, Jo thought, they don't make them like this nowadays. She felt she had stepped back into the Middle Ages.

But Solange was very real. Her haughty face relaxed into a smile as she saw Marcel, and she held out her arms to him.

'Mon cher petit-fils!'

Marcel stooped to embrace her. 'Comment vas-tu, Grand'mère?'

She said something in French and he turned to Jo.

'She would have come to welcome us, but her arthritis is troublesome today. She is a great sufferer from it.' He turned back to the old lady. 'May I introduce Mademoiselle Josephine Thornton? Josephine has only rudimentary French.'

Solange looked shocked at such ignorance, an educated girl of her class was supposed to know several languages, but she forced a smile as she said in excellent English.

'You are very welcome, ma chère. Your family and ours have been friends for many years. I hope you will enjoy your stay here.'

'I . . . I hope so too,' Jo faltered. 'It is very kind of you to have me.'

'Marcel made the arrangement,' Solange said shortly. Her tone was very cold, and her blue eyes, similar to Marcel's, were hostile. But how had she offended? She glanced reproachfully at him, wondering what he had told the old lady to earn her such a chilly welcome. She saw with surprise that Marcel was regarding his grandmother with an expression part defiance, part triumph, which suggested he had brought her in the face of opposition.

'Your horse has arrived,' Solange went on. 'An evil-looking beast, not worth what you paid for it.' Her eyes flickered disdainfully over Jo, and a dreadful idea occurred to the girl. Had her father made her banishment part of the bargain for Lucifer? He had been anxious to get her away at all costs and the reasons Marcel had given had always seemed a little thin, but he had very much wanted to acquire the horse. That he had had to be bribed to bring her hurt her pride unbearably.

'Oh yes, he is,' Marcel said carelessly, and asked where his sister was.

'Yolande Latour has returned from Italy,' he was informed. 'I sent Thérèse to St Pierre with my regards.' Marcel frowned. 'It is right and proper we should be polite to her.'

Marcel laughed. 'You never give up, do you, Grand'-mère?'

Solange said something in French and he made an impatient gesture.

'*Pas maintenant.* Josephine is tired and would like to go to her room.'

'Ring the bell for Louise. You know I cannot manage the stairs.'

He complied, and hoping to placate this formidable old woman, Jo said sympathetically:

'I'm sorry you have poor health, *madame*—arthritis, I know, is very painful.'

Solange smiled sourly. 'Until you experience it, you cannot know how much.'

The entrance of Louise cut short further conversation. She, thank goodness, looked human, Jo thought with relief. She was a round-faced country girl with a merry smile. Madame gave her some order in French, and she bobbed to the old lady, then looked expectantly at Jo.

'Run along, Josephine,' Marcel bade her. 'Louise has a smattering of English, so I daresay you can make yourself understood. I will see you at dinner.'

His manner was curt and Jo with difficulty restrained an outburst. She was angry and sore with him for putting her in such an uncomfortable position. She wanted to tell him that she could not, would not, stay where she was obviously not wanted, but she dared not speak her mind in front of his grandmother. She knew instinctively that Solange would consider any display of feeling bad manners, and for some unknown reason she had already won her displeasure.

She gave Marcel a barbed glance, and followed Louise out of the room.

CHAPTER SIX

LOUISE conducted Jo up the great staircase and along the gallery to a room looking out over the front door. The furniture was old-fashioned—a large *armoire*, dressing table and high double bed—but it looked comfortable, and had its own bathroom installed in what had once been a powder closet.

'*Voici la salle de bain*,' Louise threw open the door. 'I run him, *oui*? You *laver* . . . me, I unpack.'

'Thank you.' Jo was unused to being maided, and she wanted to say that she did not want her clothes unpacked, nor to dress for dinner, all she desired was to leave this inhospitable place, but Louise was already turning on taps and the sound of running water was inviting. Jo began to undo her waistcoat and blouse. It was too late to do anything tonight and the bath would relax her and give her time to think. If she said she was very tired, the friendly girl might bring her something on a tray and she need not face the family tonight.

Over lunch in Paris, Marcel had begun to seem like a friend and intimacy had grown between them, but if her suspicion was correct he was only putting up with her as part of the bargain made with her father to enable him to acquire the horse. She was still seething with indignation as she took off the suit that had been bought to please him. She had still to meet Thérèse, and if the sister resented her as much as the grandmother did, her situation would be quite unbearable. She must find some way of escaping from this hateful place.

Louise had filled the big, old-fashioned bath with fragrant essences, and as she soaked in it Jo's tension began to seep away. She would tell Marcel next morning that she could not stay at the château, but she would like to remain in France for a while since she was here. There must be plenty of accommodation available, and if she rang her father he would arrange to pay her expenses. The Thorntons were a proud, independent family, as much so as the de Savignys, for all their escutcheons, and he would not want her to be unwelcome and humiliated. Wrapped in a big fleecy towel, she re-entered the bedroom where Louise had put out the black dress and clean underwear. But when she said she wanted to go to bed, the maid expostulated. She would give offence if she did not go down to dine, Monsieur le Comte and his sister were expecting her and they would be '*très désolés*' if she did not appear.

'And the old lady, I don't think!' Jo said rudely.

But Madame de Savigny, it appeared, did not stay up for dinner. *Le déjeuner* was the only meal she partook with her family, the others being served in her downstairs suite.

That was good news, and Jo changed her mind. It was a long time since lunch and she was hungry, and she might have an opportunity to ring her father tonight, after she had told Marcel of her decision. So she dressed in the black frock, and Louise did her hair. Though it was only shoulder-length the French girl managed to manipulate its thick strands so that it was drawn off her face and pleated behind her head. Jo was pleased with the result, deciding she looked quite mature. There were cosmetics on the dressing table and Louise expertly added èye-shadow, and put cream and powder over the exposed part of Jo's neck and throat, but she shook her head over her tanned hands; there was nothing she could do to disguise the sunburn. Stepping back to view her handiwork, she exclaimed:

'*Mademoiselle est belle!*'

Jo surveyed herself in the cheval glass that was part of the furnishings. Hardly that, she thought, but she did look rather nice.

Louise left her and she began to regret that she had yielded to her persuasions. Would there be a gong or a bell to announce dinner, and would she be able to find the dining room?

There was a tap on her door, and without waiting for an answer a girl burst tempestuously into the room, a young woman with a thick mop of black hair reaching to her shoulders, a thin aristocratic nose, and big dark eyes. She was dressed strikingly in scarlet silk trousers and a black and scarlet tunic. She was sufficiently like her brother for Jo to surmise she was Thérèse de Savigny. She halted in the centre of the room staring at Jo.

'*Tiens*, but you are not at all what I expected. You are Miss Thornton, are you not?'

'Yes, and you are Monsieur de Savigny's sister?'

'Yes, I am Thérèse.' She continued to study Jo critically. 'I wanted to see what you were like. I feared you might be an insipid blonde. Marc likes small, fluffy women, you are not at all his usual type, and you are so young.'

'I believe I'm your age,' Jo said stiffly, wondering what misconception Thérèse was harbouring. She had learned that Marcel preferred small women, but he liked them dark.

'That is what is so strange. Marc does not care for young girls, he finds them dull.'

Jo noticed that Thérèse's English was very good. She did not need any tuition, but she had already decided that his supposed reasons for bringing her here were bogus.

'Your brother's preferences are of no interest to me . . .' she was beginning, when Thérèse interrupted her.

'No, no, you need not pretend with me, I guessed at once. Obviously Marc would not have brought you back with him unless he was interested.' She giggled. 'Grand'mère was furious when he told her you were coming. You know perhaps she has long wanted him to marry Yolande Latour, who is rich and suitable . . . and so dull! She declared you were a young adventuress who was trying to trap Marc into marriage. As if any girl could catch Marc if he did not want to be caught! I have so hoped he would take up with someone more attractive than Yo Latour. She is so conventional and prim. You are going to marry him?'

About to say she would not marry Marcel de Savigny if he were the last man on earth, Jo checked herself as the possibilities of this misunderstanding began to dawn on her. She understood now why Solange de Savigny had greeted her so coldly. She thought Marcel intended to marry her and had brought her to introduce her to his family. She blamed Jo for detaching him from his allegiance to the so-suitable heiress. Nothing could be farther from the truth, but if she deliberately fostered this error, she could put Marcel in a very awkward position. He would deny that he had had any such idea, but he *had* brought her here upon what appeared to be

very flimsy excuses. She would protest that she had mis-
understood his intentions, and he was letting her down
by repudiating her. She had not forgiven him for abet-
ting her exile from her home and his arrogant attitude
towards her. It would be amusing to pretend she
thought she was engaged to him, a retaliation for his
grandmother's cold welcome, and the role of adventuress sounded so dashing. It meant, didn't it, a woman
who was out to feather her nest at the expense of any
unwary male. Marcel might not find it easy to allay his
family's suspicions if she supported them, and she
would enjoy his discomfiture, especially if it made
trouble for him with this Yolande Latour, whom he was
keeping dangling. She had not had time to consider
how she could use the situation to her best advantage,
and it could be very much so. In the meantime she
would hedge.

'It's not definite yet,' she said, trying to look appro-
priately coy. 'We haven't known each other very long,
but I . . . I fell for him at first sight, and he for me.' She
raised anxious grey eyes to Thérèse's face. 'But this
Miss Latour . . . you've given me a shock. I didn't know
there was a prior attachment.'

'No more there is, except in Grand'mère's imagination,' Thérèse returned decisively. 'She insists they were
betrothed in their cradles, but Marc only laughs and
says he cannot honour a contract that was made before
he was old enough to know what he was doing. But Yo
wants to be a *comtesse*, her people are bankers, very
wealthy but not of the *noblesse*.' She eyed Jo doubtfully.
'Is it that you also wish to be a *comtesse*?'

'I've no desire whatever to be one,' Jo declared truthfully. 'And I thought the title had been dropped.'

'So it has, but Yo would work to have it revived.'

Jo noticed the abbreviation of Yolande's name was very like her own; perhaps that was why Marcel always called her Josephine.

Thérèse was still regarding her a little dubiously.

'It must have been a *coup de foudre* between you and Marc, to fall in love in such a short time.'

'I told you it was love at first sight,' Jo insisted, enjoying herself. The cynical Marcel would be furious to be accused of such weakness.

'I have never quite believed in it before,' Thérèse admitted, 'but it must be so. You have stars in your eyes.'

Jo turned quickly to glance in her mirror. Her eyes were sparkling, but it was with mischief, not love.

'I am very glad,' Thérèse went on. 'I did not want Marc to marry Yo, and I think you and I will do well together. Yo treats me like a child and supports Marc in refusing to allow me to live in Paris, which is what I want. Also she disapproves of my taste in dress.' She glanced at her scarlet-clad figure in the mirror. 'She says this outfit is *outré*. Do you think so?'

'No, it suits you, and you look charming.' Jo was warming to Thérèse, recognising another rebel against convention.

A knock on the door startled them. Thérèse ran to open it, throwing it wide to disclose Marcel standing on the threshold. He had changed for dinner, wearing a blue velvet jacket which enhanced the colour of his eyes. Jo's heart missed a beat at the sight of him and for a moment she regretted her rash disclosures. It seemed presumption to claim an intimate relationship with such a superior-looking being.

Thérèse threw her arms round his neck. She was nearly as tall as he was, a long slim girl.

'Ah, Marcel *chéri*, I came back from St Pierre too late to welcome you. You had gone to change.' She relapsed into voluble French.

'English, please,' Marcel told her, gently disengaging himself from her clinging arms. 'You see I have brought you a gift back from England.' He nodded towards Jo.

'Yes, and she has just told me your wonderful news,' Thérèse cried excitedly.

'Has she?' Marcel sounded indifferent, he was more interested in his sister's appearance. 'You look like an Eastern houri, *chérie*. Has Grand'mère seen you in those garments?'

Thérèse shook her head, dimpling charmingly. 'She would not appreciate them. I put them on for you, and I am sure you do. But never mind my clothes, Marc. As you see I have made myself known to your *fiancée*. *Elle est ravissante!* I shall be delighted to have her for my *belle-soeur*.'

Marcel looked taken aback, as well he might. Jo braced herself, expecting an explosion. He shot her one glance like blue lightning, and for a moment she quailed. Then she raised her chin defiantly. He would tell Thérèse she was mistaken and she was prepared to upbraid him, play the innocent maiden misled by his treacherous kisses. He could not deny that he had kissed her, thought he had meant nothing by it. Already the words were forming in her brain. 'Oh, Marcel, how can you be so cruel! You told me in the forest that you loved me and of course I thought you meant marriage.'

That he had said nothing of the sort did not matter. Thérèse would believe her and take her part.

Marcel discreetly closed the door. His action was deliberate and a little ominous. He wanted no eavesdropping upon what he was going to say.

'Josephine has been a little premature,' he said pleasantly. 'We are not yet officially betrothed.' He put his hands in his trouser pockets and eyed Jo's slim black figure with a glitter in his eyes, but his quiet voice did not betray the annoyance he must be feeling.

'I have brought her here so that she could see the château and become *au fait* with our way of life, for when we are married she will have to live here. Love is not everything, *ma petite soeur*, and she must accustom herself to an existence very different from what she has known previously. Being impetuous,' he smiled sardonically, 'she has declared that nothing could make any difference to her feelings for me, but being older and wiser I have insisted upon a . . . er . . . preparatory period before she commits herself irrevocably, and I trust she will consider well before she makes her decision. As you know, Maman hated the château, and I do not want a wife who is clamouring all the time to live in Pariss.'

He spoke with such conviction that Jo could almost believe he meant what he said, and she admired the adroit way he had handled the situation, neither denying nor admitting anything, but the only true word he had uttered was the statement that he did not want a wife, not with that dainty little mistress installed in Paris. It occurred to her that she might have given him an excuse to ward off an involvement with Yolande Latour, and that was why he had not said she was lying. That had not been her idea at all, but he had been as quick as she had been to see advantages in her deception.

'*Mon Dieu*, Marc, you do not sound like a man in love,' Thérèse exclaimed. 'Such cold-blooded reasoning!'

'I am no hot-headed youth,' he returned calmly. 'I

have to consider Josephine's happiness as well as my own. She must be quite sure she can bear to live here.'

Again a swift glance in Jo's direction, with a hint of malice in it, and she felt uneasy. He was meditating some form of reprisal, and it would probably be unpleasant. Turning to Thérèse, he went on:

'So for the present you will not permit that indiscreet little tongue of yours to wag, *chérie*. I will let you be the first to know when we are officially engaged—and you too, Josephine,' his tone hardened, 'had better guard your speech.'

'So it is a secret,' Therese said looking disappointed. '*Quel dommage!* I so wanted to see Yo's face when you introduced your *fiancée*.'

'*Une autre fois*,' he returned carelessly. 'I understand she and that dilettante brother of hers have come to dinner. It was not very considerate on Josephine's first night.'

'They invited themselves,' Thérèse explained. 'Grand'mère sent me over to St Pierre to welcome Yo upon her return from Italy, and when I mentioned that you were bringing Mademoiselle Thornton back with you for a visit, she could not wait to meet you. You know Grand'mère has told her she can come whenever she wishes.'

'Unfortunately she does not confine her attentions to Grand'mère,' Marcel said drily. 'You need not have mentioned Josephine's arrival.'

Thérèse gave a Gallic shrug. 'I saw no reason not to.' She giggled. 'I told her in answer to her questions—and oh, what a lot she asked!—that she was one of those horsey, angular *anglaises* who think only of hunting and racing. Even without your good news she will have a shock when she sees how lovely she is.'

'But I'm not . . .' Jo began, feeling a little bewildered. Her attempt to involve Marcel had been made simply to avenge herself for his and his grandmother's treatment of her, but now it seemed there would be repercussions with which it might be difficult to cope. She had not expected to be made into a stooge to ward off Yolande Latour's importunity. He was watching her with a flickering flame in his eyes that indicated suppressed anger, but she was not intimidated. She felt he had brought her here under false pretences; Thérèse did not need lessons in English nor a companion. She would have plenty to say to him when she got him alone.

'Lovely?' Marcel broke in suavely. 'You look very well, Josephine, though black is too old for you.'

His patronising tone annoyed her.

'I'll be ancient if I stay here much longer,' she retorted. 'My education in worldly knowledge is increasing by leaps and bounds.' She looked at him significantly.

'On the contrary, *mon enfant*, it has not yet begun,' he told her equally significantly.

Thérèse gave them puzzled glances. Josephine's attitude towards Marcel was not that of a girl in love, she seemed antagonistic, but she might be put out by having Yolande foisted upon her, and that was understandable.

'I think you ought to give Yo a hint,' she said to her brother. 'You are not being fair either to her or Josephine.'

'Yolande will draw her own conclusions,' he retorted. He became suddenly aware that he was in Jo's bedroom. 'I apologise for this intrusion, Josephine. I came to conduct you downstairs in case you lost your way—I did not mean to come inside, but this baggage,' he smiled affectionately at his sister, 'diverted me.'

Thérèse giggled again.

'Do not pretend you are not familiar with ladies' bedrooms, Marc, and I do not suppose you wait for an invitation to enter.' She threw a half-apologetic glance at Jo. 'My brother is a brave *homme du monde*.'

'I know that,' Jo told her.

Marcel slapped Thérèse's rear.

'And you are a *méchante enfant*. Let us go down. I suppose our guests are with Grand'mère, but it is time she retired.'

He opened the door and stood aside to allow them to precede him. Thérèse put her arm around Jo's waist and waltzed her along the gallery to the head of the stairs.

'I am so happy about you and Marc,' she murmured. 'I am sure he must love you very much.'

Jo felt ashamed of her deception. Love, she thought grimly, was the last thing Marcel felt for her.

The Latours had been dismissed by the old lady, and were being served pre-dinner drinks in the *salon*. Yolande was brown-haired, green-eyed, tall and slim, and wore a décolleté green dress. She was not pretty, her nose was too long, her eyes too close-set, but she was perfectly groomed from her lacquered head to her high-heeled shoes. Charles was a carbon copy of his sister, having paler eyes and hair and a much less forceful personality.

Marcel introduced Jo, and Yolande extended a languid hand, her sharp eyes taking in every detail of Jo's appearance.

'*Comment allez vous?*' Her voice was high and a little nasal.

'Josephine has little French,' Marcel told her.

'Ah, the insular English!' It was almost a sneer.

Yolande shrugged her bare shoulders displayed by her low-cut gown. About her neck were diamonds, far too ostentatious for an informal dinner. She laid her hand upon Marcel's sleeve. 'Where have you been hiding, *mon cher ami*? We have been waiting a long time.'

'We have had a long journey,' Marcel returned pointedly. 'It was necessary to bath and change. Josephine too is tired.'

'We could not wait to welcome you.' Yolande gave him a languishing smile that did not reach her eyes. 'After all, we are like your family.'

'Not quite,' Marcel said brusquely, and introduced Charles, who was hovering expectantly, to Jo. He immediately sought to monopolise her, not sharing his sister's antipathy.

Gaston was dispensing drinks and Jo accepted a Martini, more to have something to do than because she needed stimulating; the highly charged atmosphere was doing that. It was obvious that Marcel was not in love with Yolande; his answers to her questions were short to the point of rudeness, both of them were smouldering with suppressed anger, and Jo suspected she was the cause of it. Thérèse was bubbling with inner excitement, while Charles started paying Jo extravagant compliments, calling her an English rose and other flowery epithets. Mindful of Marcel's tuition, Jo accepted them demurely, controlling her amusement, though she longed to tell him not to be an ass. Both the Latours spoke fluent English.

Forgetting she was supposed to be an inconspicuous companion, Jo became radiant, her eyes shone and her cheeks glowed as she parried Marcel's double-edged remarks and Charles' increasing boldness. She was being quite witty, she thought happily, as Charles guffawed at one of her audacious sallies.

Gaston announced dinner and Marcel detached her from Charles with an imperious, 'Come along, Jo,' and drew her arm through his. He had used her shortened name and, thinking he meant her, Yolande had moved towards him. He left her glaring after them as he conducted Jo out of the *salon* into the hall.

'Has the devil taken possession of you?' he demanded, pressing her arm against his side.

'Like the chameleon, I take colour from my surroundings,' she retorted gaily, and Marcel pinched her fingers hard. 'Oh, you brute!'

'An expression of my love,' he returned as they entered the *salle-à-manger*. This was another large room, with heavy dark furniture. The dining table, which when fully extended could seat over a score, was pushed against one wall, and dinner was laid on a small oval one before the window. The last of the summer day lighted the sky through the uncurtained window and was augmented by two three-branched candelabra placed in the centre of the table. Gaston pulled out a chair for Jo, and as she seated herself sedately, Marcel took the place beside her, and Charles that on her other side. Yolande was on Marcel's right hand, Thérèse nearly opposite; the table being oval, there was no ceremony about their seating.

Yolande enquired about the new horse and asked if she could ride it.

'Certainly not,' Marcel told her. 'I shall race him for a season and then put him to stud. He is no lady's mount, even Jo has never ridden him.' Again he used her abbreviated name.

'Even Mademoiselle Thornton?' Yolande's tone was acid. 'Is she then an expert equestrienne?'

'Better than you are,' Marcel returned ungallantly. 'You have spoiled more than one of my horses' mouths.' He turned his head towards Jo. 'I will show you the stables in the morning and you shall choose your mount.'

Reminded of their first encounter, Jo responded with a Suffolk drawl. 'That be hully foine by me. Thank 'ee koindly, bor.'

'What language is that?' Yolande asked, raising thin arched brows.

'Dialect. I regret that Josephine delights in misrepresenting herself—a reprehensible trait that must be cured.'

A stable-boy, and now his fiancée; both must rankle. 'Is that a threat?' Jo asked with outward calm and inward trepidation.

'Take it as you wish, but I think you understand.'

She did. He meant to pay her back for her various deceptions.

Bored with this, to her, incomprehensible exchange, Yolande introduced the subject of the *bal masqué*. Since they were to wear fancy dress she would impersonate the Empress Josephine.

'She was famed for her elegance and I am sure I could represent her excellently,' she said smugly.

'I believe she had bad teeth,' from Jo the irrepressible.

'That is of no importance,' Yolande declared, displaying her own pointed ones in a forced smile.

'I bet it was to her.'

'We cannot be correct in every detail,' Charles interposed. 'I shall go as Louis *Quatorze*.' He ogled Jo. 'You could be Madame de Montespan.'

Louis' most famous—or infamous—mistress. The

implication was obvious. Jo shook her head.

'Too elaborate for me.' A pity Yolande had hogged her namesake, the Empire dress would be simple to make and inexpensive, but there were other ladies of that period, including Napoleon's sisters.

'Marcel would make a good Bonaparte,' Yolande said meditatively. Again the implication was obvious.

'I have not the right figure,' Marcel objected. 'He was a small man and portly in his latter years.'

'But you have his dignity,' Yolande purred, 'his air of command. Will you not be my consort for a night?'

Thérèse, fearing Jo would resent such a blatant advance, said quickly: 'Napoleon abandoned Josephine.' She winked at Jo. 'You could be Marie-Louise who superseded her.'

'She can if she wishes, but I will not be Napoleon,' Marcel said firmly. 'As host, I shall simply be myself.'

A chorus of dissent greeted this announcement, but he was unmoved. Again Jo admired his diplomacy.

They had been served an excellent meal, consommé, ducklings with orange sauce, a ripe Roquefort, a charlotte russe with real cream, and an assortment of fresh fruit. There was also a variety of wines, red wine to go with the duck, Saumur and Anjou, both local vintages, and the fruity Touraine Gamay, but Marcel had Jo served with a sweet rosé, Cabernet d'Anjou, suspecting she would not care for dry wine.

'Stay for a glass of port,' Marcel said to Charles as they concluded their meal. 'We will join the ladies for coffee later.'

'Stable talk?' Yolande enquired disdainfully as she rose from her seat.

'Not for your ears anyway,' Charles told her with a leer.

Thérèse took Jo's arm as she stood up a little unsteadily. She was unused to alcohol.

'More likely women,' she whispered to her as they went through the door. 'You know men.'

But Jo had no intimate experience of them except for her father and Terry, and Marcel was very different from either. He was still an enigma to her. Why had he not contradicted Thérèse when she had supposed they were engaged? In the hall Thérèse halted. 'You must be very tired, *ma chère*. If you would like to go to bed, I will make your excuses, everyone will understand.'

Jo jumped at the idea. The wine had made her sleepy and she was weary with the excitements of the day. It would be a relief not to see Marcel again that night and have to fence with him. Refreshed by a night's sleep, she would feel equal to contending with him. So she bade Yolande goodnight and Thérèse came upstairs with her. Looking back over the gallery balustrade, she saw Yolande was still standing in the hall watching her retreat with a malignant expression. She had made another enemy in addition to the formidable old lady. Perhaps together they would persuade Marcel to send her home, and after the awkward position in which she had placed him, he would be sure to agree. So she would be able to return to Greyfriars, but somehow she was no longer anxious to leave.

Thérèse told her Louise would call her in the morning and bring her *petit déjeuner* which they all took in their rooms. She put her arms round Jo's neck and kissed her.

'Goodnight, *belle-soeur*. Sleep well.'

When she had gone Jo sat down at her dressing table and stared at her image in the glass. *Belle-soeur*—sister-in-law—that she would never be, and she was regretting that she had deceived Thérèse, who was the only one to give her a friendly greeting. She pondered anew upon Marcel's strange lack of denial. It would seem he intended to make use of the situation she had created for some subtle purpose of his own and she was caught in a web of her own weaving. Throughout the day he had been a considerate and stimulating companion, but that was only his courtesy towards a guest. He had told her father she was to be treated as one of the family, but he would never dream of making her a member of it. He was involved with another woman, and when that liaison was finished, he would probably marry Yolande to please his grandmother and embark upon further illicit relationships. It was the accepted pattern of French marriages, according to what she had read, for marriage to them was only a business contract which did not include love.

Why did she feel so depressed at the prospect? Marcel's amours were no concern of hers. Unwillingly she was forced to admit that he attracted her strongly, and she would very much like to win his regard. He had kissed her once with fervour, but that had been merely *pour passer le temps*, and she had struck him. Not an endearing gesture, but what was it he had said while the nightingale sang and he had put his arm around her? That he was glad she was not repelled by his touch? They had drawn closer that night in every sense, but it was merely French gallantry.

Jo sighed as she stood up and started to undress. In the morning Marcel would probably tell her she was becoming a nuisance and he would arrange to send her home.

CHAPTER SEVEN

BEING tired, Jo slept much later than she usually did, and was awakened by Louise, who said she would bring her breakfast as soon as she had bathed. When she had gone, Jo reflected that she might be wronging him by attributing unworthy motives to Marcel for bringing her to the château. Thérèse really did need companionship, for she must be very much alone, with Madame de Savigny spending most of her time in her suite and Marcel frequently absent. The nearest neighbours were the Latours, but Yolande's interest was focused on the brother and she was nearer his age than the much younger sister. As for Charles, he was a nonentity and unlikely to appeal to a lively girl like Thérèse. Jo herself felt lonesome as she sat down to her coffee and croissants, she missed the conviviality of the Greyfriars' kitchen, where from early morning onwards there was always someone coming in or going out. The thick walls of the château excluded all sound, and it was deadly quiet. She would have welcomed a radio or transistor, but she did not possess the latter, and she had yet to discover if there was any wireless or television at the château.

Thérèse came bounding in dressed for riding before Jo had finished. Marcel was waiting to show her round the stables, she said and afterwards they would *se promener à cheval*—her brother had told her to speak French to their guest.

'It will be necessary that you are fluent when you are mistress here,' she exclaimed.

Reminded of her masquerade, Jo blushed, which Thérèse took to be maidenly confusion at the thought of her nuptials.

'You will decide to marry him, will you not?' she asked coaxingly. 'Life here *n'est pas désagréable.*'

'I refuse to be rushed,' Jo hedged, forcing a laugh. The reckoning with Marcel was still to come.

'You need not always stay here,' Thérèse ran on. 'Marc has a flat in Paris, but he says I may not stay there unchaperoned, he will not even allow me to visit it, but I can come with you when you are a married lady.'

Marcel's love nest, Jo thought wryly; he would not want Thérèse butting in.

The stables were as new and modern as the château was old and shabby. Shielded from the house by a screen of trees and bushes, the stalls and boxes were ranged round a square yard with a large stone drinking trough in the centre. Marcel showed them where Lucifer was accommodated, looking none the worse for his journey. He whinnied in recognition when Jo spoke to him. He was something from home and Jo felt a wave of nostalgia as she caressed his velvet muzzle. But it vanished when as she re-entered the yard, a smart groom led out a palomino mare, a beautiful creature with a coat like gold silk and a silver mane and tail.

'Try her,' Marcel said to Jo, and held the stirrup for her to put her foot in it. Jo swung herself into the saddle and walked the animal round the yard. She moved with a light springing gait, and needed only a touch of the rein to guide her.

'She's lovely,' she said to Marcel as he came up to

her. Pleasure brightened her eyes, and her mouth was soft and tremulous. She looked lovely too, and there was something in Marcel's vividly blue eyes as he looked up at her that caused her heart to flutter, but all he said was:

'Thérèse will show you some of the countryside.'

'Aren't you coming with us?' She was disappointed.

'I have some business to attend to, but I will be here when you return. I have something to say to you, Josephine.'

'Perhaps I don't want to hear it,' she said pertly, knowing she was in for a scolding.

'*Eh bien*, that will be too bad, but I am not going to let you off.'

'That will be something to look forward to.' She would not let him see she was alarmed, and her eyes held a challenge as she met his squarely.

'Brazen minx,' he said below his breath as Thérèse, mounted on a bay gelding, came up to them. Together they left the yard.

They rode north, away from the river, through winding lanes and little rustic villages. On the southern slopes of rising ground there were vineyards and orchards. Thérèse pointed out St. Pierre, a modern building built château-style but ugly and garish, with formal gardens laid out around it. Soon it was lost in trees, as they cantered over a stretch of heath land. Above them was the vast firmament, where billowing clouds sailed before the breeze. The sky always seems immense above the valley of the Loire. The valley itself is fertile, but narrow, the land on either side is in parts bare plateaux, the soil poor, but grapes do not care for richness. There are still acres of forest. Jo asked about the châteaux for which the district was so famous, and Thérèse told her they were strung out along the river for many miles, having originally been approached by boat. Now there was a road, more or less following the river's course, but it was thronged with traffic in the tourist season.

'The *canaille*,' Thérèse wrinkled her patrician nose. 'We avoid them as much as possible.'

Superior aristocrats, thought Jo, did Thérèse realise that she was of the *bourgeoisie*?

Marcel was waiting for them when they re-entered the yard, and their horses were taken away by grooms. He noticed Jo's wistful look—she would have liked to have tended her mount herself—and laughed.

'No unsaddling and grooming for you here, *ma chère*. Come and look at my young stock.'

She hung back, and he took her elbow in a firm grip, piloting her the way he wanted her to go. Thérèse tactfully disappeared. Marcel led her to an enclosed paddock where several yearlings were grazing. Shrubs concealed it from house and stables. Jo leaned against the fence, but did not really see them; she was too conscious of the man lounging beside her. He was more casually dressed than she had ever seen him before; in corded pants, and a short-sleeved open-necked shirt, he looked lean, bronzed, debonair and . . . dangerous.

'You are a rash young woman,' he told her pleasantly. 'What exactly was your motive in telling Thérèse we were engaged?'

Jo drooped her head and drew her fingers absently along the wooden rail.

'It was just a crazy impulse,' she admitted frankly. 'It seemed Thérèse had reached that conclusion before I said anything. She and your grandmother were convinced I was out to catch you.' The absurdity of that supposition struck her afresh and she laughed, turning

to him with merriment in her eyes. 'Madame de Savigny
told Thérèse I was an adventuress.'

There was no answering amusement in his face.

'*Eh bien*, you should have undeceived her.'

'Do you always do what you should?' she countered.
'I thought it was rather a joke, so I played up to her,
but I didn't realise she was taking it seriously, and you
came in before I could rectify her error.'

There was no need to tell him she had not tried. He
said stiffly:

'Surely you resented being called an adventuress?'

Jo gave him her gamine grin. 'Not at all, I thought it
was rather fun.'

He came closer. 'Your notions of fun are a little dangerous. Hence the episode at the Pelican.'

She threw back her head defiantly. She was bare-
headed, and the sunlight turned her hair to copper, her
long throat was creamy above the V of her shirt, and
there was provocation in every line of her slim, taut
body.

'You'll never let me forget that, will you? Am I still
supposed to be wallowing in gratitude for your timely
rescue—which I believe was more for Daddy's sake
than for mine? But to return to the present, why on
earth didn't you tell your sister there was no engagement? You can be forthright enough when you please.'

'That would not have been very pleasant for you.'
She stared at him in surprise; that explanation would
never have occurred to her. 'When a hitherto un-
approachable lady does me the honour of declaring she
is affianced to me, it would be churlish to give her the
lie.'

Jo would have appreciated his chivalrous action if it
had not been spoilt by the derisive note in his voice and

the mocking glint in his eyes.

'Oh, cut out the fancy lingo,' she said crossly, then realising she was being ungrateful, she went on more gently, 'Thank you for your consideration, which I didn't deserve, but I'm afraid that rigmarole about getting used to life at the château, etc., etc. won't help.'

'Help what?'

'Extricating ourselves from the impasse, and if you expect poor Thérèse to be able to hold her tongue, you're an optimist.'

He shrugged his shoulders.

'She will not betray a secret, but she may embarrass you by her expectations.'

'What on earth do you mean?'

'That she will be on the lookout for loverlike demonstrations.' He slid his arm around her and drew her against him. 'I told you you were rash, Jo. Has it not occurred to you that a fiancé has certain privileges? You have deliberately put me in an awkward situation, but there are compensations. Being a mere man, I intend to make the most of my opportunities.'

'Oh, no!' Jo tried to free herself, but his hold tightened.

'In less permissive times, an engagement used to be called a kissing licence,' he murmured, and his mouth came down on hers. His hands moved caressingly over her back and shoulders, then he crushed her against him, and his lips wandered over her face and throat, kissing her eyelids, then settled on her mouth again, becoming hard and demanding.

Jo relaxed in his arms as the emotions he had formerly aroused in her welled up and submerged her. But this time she had no will to resist. She wanted him to go on kissing her for ever. Dazedly she thought this must be love. She had never experienced such sensations before and she was no longer outraged by the liberties he was taking. Impatiently he pulled down the front zip of her shirt, and his mouth sought the tender curve of her breasts. Her own arms were about his neck, striving to draw him even closer. One of the colts, hoping for sugar, came up to the fence and pushed an eager nose against Marcel's shoulder. That seemed to recall him to sanity. He released Jo so suddenly, thrusting away her clinging arms, that she staggered against the fence, trembling in every limb, while she held on to it for support. Marcel too seemed to be affected; he was breathing fast, his nostrils flared, his eyes alight. When he did speak his voice was unsteady.

'You go to my head, like strong wine.'

Mechanically Jo pulled up her zip and tried to smooth her ruffled hair. The colt nudged her.

'This fellow seems to have expectations too,' she said, pleased to notice her voice sounded normal.

'Ah yes.' Marcel fumbled in his pocket and produced a lump of sugar, which from past experience the animal knew he would be carrying. 'This creature is a special pet, his dam was the horse you rode this morning.'

The small incident gave Jo time to recover her equilibrium. As Marcel dismissed the colt with a pat and a brief, '*C'est tout pour le moment,*' she asked bluntly:

'Are you aiming to seduce me?'

He looked shocked, exclaiming involuntarily:

'*Mon Dieu, non!* Our old friend's daughter!'

'Well, you're going the right way about it.'

A wicked gleam came into his eyes.

'Do you perhaps want to be seduced?'

Jo looked away over the green pasture, the grazing animals which the colt had rejoined. Her profile was cameo-pale; clear-cut against the background of dark shrubs, she looked young, vulnerable and a little sad.

'No,' she said quietly, 'I want to be loved.'

'Ah, *ma chère*, love is a very different story. It is something very precious and it does not come to everyone.'

'Not to you, evidently,' she retorted a little bitterly. 'You don't love your women, do you, Marcel? You only desire them.'

'What is wrong with that?' he retorted. 'It is a natural urge between men and women, but, *ma petite*, do not confuse it with *la grande passion*. What I awoke in you was your dormant senses, too long unstirred—that was all.'

She looked at him thoughtfully, wondering if he could be right. He probably was; he was so much more experienced than she was in matters of the heart. Her words had been a spontaneous reaction to his lovemaking, a desire for reciprocation, an assurance that he felt as she did, but he was telling her that it was not love that had flared up between them, and as regarded himself she feared it was only too true. Her own feelings were a different matter; she had been too deeply stirred to take them lightly, and for the first time in her life she was in love. Marcel had the outward seeming to inspire romantic love and more than his share of sexual magnetism, both her sisters had felt it, and he had left behind him a fading dream in both their minds. But he was very much a reality to her, and she had admitted to herself only last night that her feelings towards him had changed. The strength of her response to him had alarmed her, but it would be fatal to cherish this unfortunate love, for he was only playing with her, indulging his natural urge as he had expressed it. That phrase stung her, because instinctively she knew that what had been born in her was something much deeper.

'Thank you for your explanation,' she said drily, 'but what do you propose to do about our present dilemma?'

He raised his brows quizzically. 'I fail to see the necessity to do anything but allow circumstances to take their course, which at the moment is very satisfactory.'

She flashed back at him, 'If you mean by that you intend to continue with this bogus engagement so that you'll have an excuse to pounce on me whenever you feel inclined . . .'

He cut her short. 'I have no such purpose. My actions were entirely unpremeditated, aroused by your continued provocation.' His blue eyes were full of mischief, as he added slyly, 'You did not appear to find my embrace distasteful.'

Jo flushed fierily, and was quite unable to meet his gaze. Marcel laughed triumphantly. 'So you cannot deny it.'

'But please don't make a habit of it,' she said anxiously.

'I can promise you that. When experiences become a habit they are no longer amusing.'

Anger and indignation boiled up in her. That was all she was to him—a diversion that he would abandon when it became stale.

'Oh, I hate you, Marcel de Savigny!' she cried fiercely. 'You tread on people's feelings with no thought but for your own gratification. You make us all dance to your tune—me, Thérèse, Miss Latour, even your grandmother; she believes you're going to marry Miss Latour.' She looked at him uncertainly. 'Perhaps you will in the end?'

'Certainly I must marry eventually,' he told her, the animation dying out of his face. 'But not yet, there are several matters to be resolved first.' Then he smiled impishly. 'I am not devastated by your hate, *ma chère*, for hate is the reverse side of love. I would be much more concerned if you were indifferent.'

'I don't think you're concerned about *my* feelings at all.'

'You are mistaken. I find them very . . . interesting.'

'Thank you—you make me feel like a beetle being dissected!'

But he had given her food for thought. Was it possible that the aversion she had first felt for him had been the beginning of love? Had she instinctively sought to combat an emotion which would mean succumbing to his domination? She could only gain heartache and loss from loving Marcel, for when he was tired of stalling he meant to marry that unpleasant green-eyed girl for the sake of her dowry and to beget an heir.

'Not a beetle,' he objected, as they began to move towards the house. 'I would dislike to liken you to anything so obnoxious. You should know that a Frenchman's mind is analytical, particularly where the emotions are involved.'

'That sounds damn cold-blooded!' she exclaimed heatedly.

'You know I am not.'

Jo blushed and was silent. They had come within sight of the windows of the house, and Marcel linked her arm with his.

'For appearances' sake.'

'I shall tell Thérèse it was all a mistake,' she declared.

'She may not believe you. *Alors*, Jo, you have made a

good beginning to your adventuress career. You have managed to annex the owner of the château, if only temporarily.'

'Only through your connivance, and I hate deceit.'

'Let it ride for the present. Later on you can say you cannot bear life at the château and go home. I left you that loophole, you will remember.'

'It would be better if I went home now.'

'That I cannot allow.' He smiled wickedly. 'You cannot leave without my permission, and I have your passport.'

Damn him, so he has, she thought angrily, for he had taken charge of her travel documents.

'I will only cause everyone embarrassment if I stay longer,' she insisted.

'Far from it, and I promised your father you should stay until you had forgotten Terry Robinson.'

She had not thought of Terry since she had left England.

'You know perfectly well there was nothing between him and me.'

'I never thought there was, but your father did. Stay until after the *fête* anyway. You will enjoy that.'

Jo considered that was unlikely, but she was reluctant to leave the château and this enigmatical man who still held her arm, though she knew continued contact with him could only cause her heartbreak.

'It seems I'll have to,' she remarked ungraciously, 'but if you're keeping me here to annoy Miss Latour, you're being mean. Is it necessary to try to make her jealous?'

'Not Yolande,' he retorted cryptically as they entered the house.

Madame de Savigny joined them for lunch and was

coldly courteous to Jo, asking if she had enjoyed her ride and if she were comfortable in her room. The meal finished, she asked Jo—it was more like a command— to accompany her to her suite. The small sitting room in the base of one of the towers was semi-circular in shape and overcrowded with what were evidently Solange's favourite pieces and knick-knacks. There she put Jo through a catechism about her family and its prospects.

'Three daughters!' Madame pursed her lips. 'If your father has only his farm their *dots* cannot be large.'

Jo suppressed a smile at the old-fashioned word.

'Englishmen don't expect dowries,' she said. 'Jess and Ally will marry, I expect, but I shall stay with Dad. I'm learning to run the farm.'

'Then why have you come here?'

'Thérèse . . .'

'Bah!' Madame snapped her bony fingers. 'Do you expect me to credit that Marc would bring a girl over-seas under his personal escort for his sister's benefit? A girl who uses his first name and treats him as an equal? You have an unusual kind of beauty, *mademoiselle*, and plenty of spirit. Marc is susceptible, but you are not a suitable bride for him, whatever your aspirations. Do you imagine you could step into my shoes?'

'They'd pinch me horribly,' Jo admitted with a gamine grin, but Solange was not amused. 'You're mis-taken, *madame*,' she went on. 'There's nothing but friendship between me and your grandson.'

'Do not seek to pull wool over my eyes. Friendship! Bah, there is no such thing between man and woman. Marc must marry Yolande, she has the money to re-novate the château.' She looked lovingly round the room where carpets and curtains were a little shabby. 'She will restore it to all its ancient glory. Perhaps Marc has told you he does not care about it, but as he grows older he will come to appreciate it. It was the cradle of his ancestors, and will be that of his sons, but *hélas*, its upkeep costs more and more. Yolande will make it secure, and she will bring up her children to love and reverence their great heritage.'

Jo realised that the château was Madame's great love. To it she would sacrifice Marcel's happiness and anything else that stood in her way to ensure its possession in perpetuity.

'Do you believe stones and mortar are more important than happiness?' she asked curiously.

'Yes, because they endure, while happiness is ephemeral. But I cannot expect a *parvenue* like yourself to understand our great traditions.'

'Perhaps not,' Jo agreed, 'but I think they're outdated.'

Solange looked disgusted. 'Like most moderns you have no reverence for the past.' The blue eyes narrowed, needle-sharp, 'Perhaps you are also permissive, as they call it?'

'Not more than most,' Jo told her, repressing a hot denial. Since the old lady was determined that she had designs upon Marcel, she would not try to reassure her; she did not deserve it. She wondered uneasily if Thérèse had been indiscreet, thus fostering Solange's suspicions.

'Mademoiselle Latour is much incensed by your arrival,' Madame went on, 'she considers your presence is an insult to her.'

'I can't help it if Marcel didn't consult her,' Jo retorted. 'And her attitude is an insult to me.'

'She sees the obvious.'

'There's nothing to see.' Tired of these insinuations,

Jo looked straight into the hard eyes, and added: 'I came here because my father and your grandson arranged it over my head. As far as I know the reasons you've been given are correct, but I'll tell you this, Marcel has every right to marry whom *he* pleases, and if he should choose me, I'd feel honoured.'

She knew there was no possibility of that, but she wanted to needle this old harridan, and her words had the ring of truth.

'Mon Dieu!' The wrinkled face became a mask of fury. 'He cannot, he must not!' She struggled to her feet. 'Go to your room!' Her voice became shrill. 'You are an obstinate, scheming hussy, and I would sooner see you dead than mistress of Savigny!'

Melodrama, Jo thought, as she sped thankfully from the room, but in the passage she halted. Madame was old and such passion was bad for her. She might have a stroke or a heart attack. Someone should go to her. Opportunely, Marcel appeared coming towards her.

'Hullo,' he hailed her. 'Confidences over?'

'Marc!' Unconsciously she used the name the family called him by. 'Please go to her, she's upset.'

His black brows drew together. 'What have you been saying to her?'

'It's what she said to me—she was rude and insulting.'

His head went up. 'My grandmother is never discourteous.' He gave her a keen glance. 'Were you playing your adventuress act?'

'No . . . yes . . . please go to her, Marc.'

He went swiftly down the passage to knock on Solange's door. Jo sought the solitude of her own room, and sat down on the bed, trying to recollect all she had said to Madame de Savigny. Nothing, she decided, that could be distorted if relaid to Marcel, even with embellishments. He was probably well aware of the old lady's attitude. Not that the situation was not complicated enough without Madame's intervention. She had misled Thérèse into believing she was secretly engaged to her brother, and he had refused to deny it. Yolande Latour, suspecting an involvement, was jealous, and jealous women could be spiteful. Madame de Savigny, convinced there was an involvement, was breathing fire and brimstone. Even Jo's courage had faltered before the venom in her face when she had dismissed her.

It would all be rather amusing if her heart had not been affected, but somewhere along the line she had lost it to Marcel, who did not want it. That made her vulnerable to all the unpleasant innuendoes flung at her, and worse still, Marcel was inclined to make capital out of the position in which she had placed herself, by making mock love to her. Jo gave a long sigh as she pushed her fingers ruefully through her hair. How peaceful existence at Greyfriars seemed compared with the intrigues at the château! Perhaps Madame de Savigny would prevail upon Marcel to let her go home, but even that prospect did not please her. It would mean she would never see him again, and that thought filled her with despair.

What passed between Marcel and his grandmother Jo never knew. In answer to her enquiry as to her health, he assured her she was perfectly all right, but he gave her a very odd look, and she wondered what Solange had said to him. For the present she was doing as he had advised, letting things slide. She had letters from home, both her sisters writing with messages for Marcel, which she dutifully delivered and he received with a sardonic smile. Did he have any idea of the havoc he wrought in feminine breasts? she thought resentfully.

June had passed into July and preparations were going forward for Thérèse's party. Jo had procured a length of muslin and Louise, who was a good needle-woman, which Jo was not, was running up a simple Empire gown for her to wear. She rode with Thérèse most mornings, and in the afternoons they visited some of the nearer châteaux—Blois, Chambord, and the great mediaeval castle at Sully-sur-Loire. This is complete, with moat, parapets, curtain wall and towers crowned with pepperpot roofs, which are the trademark of this period's architecture. It dates from 1363, and it was from here that Jeanne d'Arc rode out in 1430 on her last expedition which led to her capture. To Jo's relief, Madame de Savigny developed a slight indisposition—or was it temper?—and kept to her own suite so that Jo had no contact with her.

For more distant expeditions, Marcel insisted that he or Charles go with them. The road that follows the river through Orleans, Touraine and Anjou to the borders of Brittany, a distance of nearly two hundred miles, is congested in the season, and he did not like Thérèse driving too far alone without a relief chauffeur. Jo had not yet learned to drive. The châteaux are strung like jewels on a chain along the river, though not all are on its banks, but on those of lesser streams. Jo soon realised that Savigny was a very minor erection compared with the other great piles she visited. The nobility deserted the Loire before the Revolution when Louis XIV built Versailles and hunted in Fontainebleau, which was much nearer to his capital. Marcel insisted that Jo ought to see all the major edifices, and some of them entailed an all-day excursion. She had no great love of stately homes, and might have rebelled except that she enjoyed the outing and the weather was beautiful. But her head was soon whirling with impressions of turreted buildings, magnificently furnished rooms, and the formal laid out gardens.

The Château of Chenonceaux is one of the best known, and Jo thought it was deservedly so. Marcel took them that day, using his big car instead of Thérèse's Fiat, for it was a long journey. It is remarkable for the two-storeyed gallery running out over the river Cher, a tributary of the Loire, with a huge square of formalised garden in front of it, the whole enclosed in a bower of trees and woods. Marcel informed Jo that it had at one time belonged to Diane de Poitiers, as a present from her lover, Henri II.

'Because of that it will always be linked with beauty and romantic love,' he told her solemnly.

'In which you don't believe,' she retorted.

'That is untrue. I warned you that other emotions could be mistaken for it.'

They were standing in the garden with the lovely Renaissance building before them. There was a brief lull in the thronging tourists and for a moment they were alone.

'I wish we could have our *bal masqué* here,' Thérèse said. 'It cries out for the brocade and velvets of former days. Trousers and blouses are all wrong. Why do you not come to my party as Henri II, Marc? Jo could be Diane, it would be so appropriate.'

'Not at all. Joe is not my mistress,' Marcel said shortly.

'Near enough.' Thérèse was eager. 'As Charles said, we cannot be correct in every detail.'

Marcel laughed, shrugged and turned away as a fresh gang of sightseers came pouring across the garden.

In actual fact, Diane was made to exchange Chenonceaux for Chaumont by Catherine de Medicis, the vengeful widow of her royal lover, and it was Catherine who added the gallery running out over the river. She was deeply associated with the Loire valley, and all the Valois masques and fêtes, the shadows of which still people the woods, waters and formal gardens, and were instigated by her.

They had lunch at an unpretentious inn, and then Marcel drove south to visit other châteaux. The castle at Loches, he told Jo, was impregnated with memories of Agnès Sorel, a local girl, who found a king's favour. Then he decided they had had enough history for one day and made for Vouvray for 'refreshment', for there numerous producers offer the opportunity of sampling the most famous of all the Loire wines both in its still and sparkling form to visitors to their cellars. Thérèse and Jo joined in this orgy, which Jo decided afterwards was responsible for her subsequent reckless behaviour.

It was getting dark when they left Vouvray and drove through Amboise on their way home. Its château standing high above the roofs of the town was floodlit, its towers and arches looking like those of a fairy palace.

As Jo looked at it, a daring idea occurred to her. Several kings had housed their mistresses along the Loire—homes of beauty and romantic love. Savigny also could be that. By her own request she was sitting in the rear of the car and Marcel's well shaped dark head was in front of her. It dominated her thoughts. She was weary of frustration, half-truths and evasions; it was time something definite emerged. She knew she could, in modern parlance, turn him on; could she not for once use that power for her satisfaction instead of his? He might pretend he had scruples, but she had none at all. All this talk of love and mistresses was tantalising.

She did not believe she would ever marry, but she could have one precious memory to take back with her from the Loire to cherish for the rest of her life. All that she needed was the courage to take the initiative, and she had never been a coward. She smiled gleefully to herself as the car sped along the busy road. She would give Marcel de Savigny a big surprise!

CHAPTER EIGHT

MARCEL came in to dinner that night without having changed and in a flaming temper. They had arrived back late after their long expedition and as usual he had made his nightly round of the stables before dressing for the meal, and some catastrophe must have occurred to make him so late. Thérèse glanced at his black brows drawn down over smouldering blue eyes and asked timidly:

'Is something wrong?'

'That damned fool Jacques!' Marcel snapped.

Jacques Dubois was a groom who had lived all his working life at Savigny and was devoted to horses, but he had one weakness—the bottle. There had been instant rapport between him and the black stallion, so that Marcel, overlooking the previous lapse, had given him sole charge of the animal, because most of the other men were afraid of him.

'He allowed Lucifer to break loose,' Marcel went on, 'being, I suppose, drunk. The horse rampaged all over the countryside, and we have only just managed to corner him. Luckily he will come to me when he will not permit anyone else near him, except Jacques, who was *hors de combat*.'

'He's not hurt?' Jo enquired anxiously.

'Lucifer? Not noticeably. He was in Jourdain's meadow—where he grazes that mare of his. Delicacy forbids a further description of what was happening.'

'So no harm's done,' said Jo, relieved.

'Oh, none at all, except that I do not import valuable stallions to service my neighbour's miserable stock.'

'Cannot you charge him for it?' Thérèse asked.

'He would not pay, in fact he is threatening me with a demand for compensation for damage to his fences. Naturally I dismissed Jacques on the spot.'

'*Oh, non,* you will break his heart!' Thérèse exclaimed. 'Savigny is his whole life.'

'He has become unreliable,' Marcel told her tersely. 'I cannot keep him on the place.'

How implacable he is, Jo thought. Jacques Dubois had aged in his and his father's service, but he had no mercy on him.

The excellent dinner and rich Angevin wine restored Marcel's temper, and he remarked that Jacques would be entitled to a pension, but the condition attached to it must be that he keep out of the stable yard, which would hardly be adequate compensation, since horses were the old man's life. Thérèse said:

'Jacques is a vengeful old man, Marc, you had better be on your guard.'

Marcel laughed contemptuously, holding up his glass to the light which shone through the liquid turning it to the colour of blood.

'You read too many thrillers, *ma chère.* What could a weasel of a man like Jacques do to me?'

It occurred to Jo that he had used an unfortunate simile, for weasels are killers, but preoccupation with her own problems soon caused the incident to fade from her mind. The daring project that had occurred to her while meditating upon the history of Diane, Agnès, Pompadour and co. caused her eyes to brim with wickedness, and Marcel, glancing at her, demanded sharply:

'What devilry are you hatching now, madcap?'

'Wait and see,' she returned demurely.

'*Eh bien*, if you cause me any further annoyance tonight I will not be responsible for my actions.'

Thérèse looked from one to the other with a bewildered air.

'You two are not like *amoureux*,' she complained. 'You behave more as if you were enemies.'

'Lovers often are enemies,' Marcel declared cryptically. He threw Jo a lowering glance. 'The result of frustration.'

'Then you ought to get married soon,' Thérèse suggested.

Marcel gave a mock sigh. 'If only we could! But Josephine has not yet made up her mind.'

'Oh, Jo!' Thérèse's dark eyes were full of reproach. 'You are cruel to keep my poor brother in suspense.'

'He seems to be bearing up under it very well,' Jo retorted. She met Marcel's blue gaze with bravado and was surprised to notice the flicker of flame in his eyes.

'I am adept at concealing my emotions, Thérèse, and the English miss is taught to restrain hers. Being unnaturally and unusually cautious, Jo is taking a long time to make up her mind.' He gave her a barbed glance and added piously, 'I am sure her decision will be the right one.'

Then, bored with teasing his supposed fiancée, Marcel changed the subject.

Since they were all tired after the day-long expedition, they did not linger in the *salon* after coffee. Marcel went to say goodnight to his grandmother, who rarely slept before midnight, and the girls went upstairs. Jo's bedroom was over the front door; Marcel and Thérèse, she had discovered, were lodged on either side of her, though there was an empty guest room between hers and that occupied by the master of the château. All their doors opened on to the gallery. The servants slept among the maze of small rooms over the back premises, and Madame de Savigny and her personal maid occupied the downstairs suite at the far end of the building.

Jo bathed and put on a nightgown instead of her usual pyjamas. It was a flimsy nylon affair that Alison had given her one Christmas and her mother had packed in her luggage. She had smiled scornfully when she had discovered it. Her relatives were always trying to encourage her to appear more feminine, but now she was glad that she had it. There was a scent spray on the dressing table, Thérèse had put it there, and Jo used it lavishly. Then she went to the long glass inset in the wardrobe and studied herself critically. Did she look seductive? Her reflection showed a tall, long-legged figure, draped in soft nylon folds, her small bosom nicely rounded but not conspicuous. Her skin had the creamy texture of a magnolia blossom, and was white where it had not been exposed to the sun; but her neck and arms were tanned. Patchy like a skewbald horse, she thought disconsolately, recalling Alison's efforts with sun-tan lotion. She saw the point of that now, though at the time she had been scornful of her sister's efforts. Her hair seemed to glow with a life of its own, but it was too red, and not everyone admired red hair. She turned away with a little sigh, seeing in her mind's eye a stylish Parisienne, a petite brunette with the bosom and hips of a fully developed woman, for so she envisioned Marcel's *bien-aimée*. True, she had an advantage over Yolande in looks, but even Yolande had more style. She sat down on her bed feeling depressed and her eyes fell on a framed photograph of her father which she had brought with her. The pictured eyes met hers reproachfully.

The marriage of Roger and Annette Thornton had been a very happy one, and Annette was a one-man woman; there had been no one else in her life besides her husband. Her brood of daughters, imbued with modern freedoms, had caused her some anxiety, but she had striven by love and understanding to maintain her influence over them, and in that she had had her husband's support. Both knew that restrictions and homilies were useless. Jo was the most wayward of the trio, and her adventurous spirit had led her into many scrapes, but always she had known her parents were her friends and standby, especially her father. Now, faced with the most traumatic experience of her young life, she was separated from home and family, and by sending her away, she felt her father had somehow failed her. Had he been there, she would have gone to him to straighten out the tangle in which she found herself, but now she had no one to whom to turn.

Her love for Marcel was the most powerful emotion she had ever experienced, it was totally unexpected and overwhelming, but she was sure he would never dream of marrying her. Her ardent spirit could not face the possibility of no fulfilment, she was no wilting lily, but a girl who did something about it. Both the incidents in the forest and the paddock had indicated that there was an affinity between them, though in Marcel's case it was only physical attraction. But it would be sufficient to ensure for her a rapturous reception if she went to him tonight. On the principle that half a loaf was better than no bread she would take what he had to offer and not consider the painful aftermath, for he would not want a permanent connection. Considering consequences had never been Jo's strong point.

Then she met her father's pictured eyes again and knew she could not do it. She could never face him again with such a secret between them, knowing how shocked and dismayed he would be if she told him what she had done. He trusted Marcel and he trusted her, and not only would she be betraying his trust in her, but she would be inciting Marcel to do likewise. There were greater loyalties than her passion for the Frenchman, who had no real love for her, and would certainly cease to respect her if she followed out her intention of going to him tonight. She nodded ruefully at the photograph.

'Okay, Daddy, you win. I guess I wasn't cut out to be a courtesan.'

Those royal mistresses who had so inspired her to emulation had, after all, given themselves more for gain than love. Diane de Poitiers had obtained Chenonceaux from Henri II, the lover twenty years her junior, and it had been a magnificent token of his favour. At least there was nothing mercenary about her own love for Marcel. She expected nothing from him, and Savigny was destined to be Yolande's home. All she wanted from Marcel was his love, and that was bestowed elsewhere.

Feeling deflated, she wandered over to the window, drew the curtain aside and looked out. There was a bright moon and the terrace before the château was fully illuminated by its silver rays. Beneath Marcel's window a man was standing looking up at it. He was small and insignificant, but in spite of that there was something sinister about him, an aura of hate which caused Jo's sensitive nerves to vibrate. He seemed to be

holding something . . . a stick or what? All the lurid
newspaper stories of shot gun murders flashed into her
brain. The man was Jacques, and Thérèse had warned
that he was vindictive. Was he contemplating climbing
up to the window? The little man was agile as a monkey
and the worn stonework of the façade would afford him
footholds. Marcel must be alerted. Without pausing to
put on her dressing gown, Jo rushed out of her room
and down the corridor towards his. His door was un-
locked and she burst in without knocking, glancing
fearfully towards the window, outside which the assas-
sin might at any moment appear.

'Marcel . . .' she began, and stopped, for the room
was empty.

It was furnished very similarly to hers, except that the
bed was wider and it contained an upholstered arm-
chair. It was dimly lit, for only the bedside light was on,
and the far corners were shadowy. The lamp illuminated a photograph by his bed, and she glanced at it
curiously, expecting to see a female portrait. It was, but
the lady was his grandmother.

There was evidence that Marcel had been in the
room, for his jacket was thrown across the bed and his
shoes were in the middle of the floor. Then she heard
the sound of running water and realised that he too had
his own bathroom and was performing his ablutions. Jo
hesitated, wondering if she dared creep up to the
window and see if Jacques were still there. Marcel was
in the bathroom, but he might appear at any moment
. . . naked. His looking-glass reflected her image, looking wraithlike and insubstantial in the dim light,
swathed in her nylon drapery.

The bathroom door opened, and Marcel stood on the
threshold, clad only in black pyjama trousers. Smooth

brown torso and powerful shoulders gleamed like bronze in the subdued lighting. He had very little hair on his chest, and his damp locks curled about his patrician head attractively, while his eyes gleamed like sapphires as he beheld his visitor.

For a fraction of time they stared at each other, then, overcome with desperate shyness, Jo drooped her bright head, her warning forgotten, overwhelmed by a surge of passionate longing. Her hair was the only colour about her, for her face was pale as alabaster, and the pastel shade of her nightdress had a ghostly effect.

Then, swift as a panther pouncing upon its prey, Marcel moved. Reaching her, he dropped to his knees, clasping her thighs with both his arms, his head pressed against her abdomen. Jo forgot Jacques, her father, Yolande, everything except Marcel's presence and the triumph of having brought him to his knees. Her hands moved over his hair, then caressed his naked shoulders.

In one swift movement he released his hold and was on his feet again, gathering her close against him, raining kisses on her face and lips, and she responded, sinking against him, weak with love, her bones seeming to melt, as they strove to weld themselves ever closer together.

It was the scent that destroyed those idyllic moments. Marcel suddenly wrinkled his nose and pushed her almost violently away from him.

'Faugh! *Quelle horreur!*'

'What is it?'

'That . . . stink!'

'It is called Allure, it is some Thérèse lent me.'

'*Eh bien,* it does not allure me.'

The spell was broken and consternation gathered in Marcel's face. He passed a hand over his eyes as if to dispel a dream, and his voice was harsh as he exclaimed:

'So you are real! I thought you were a phantom evoked by my longing. So often I have imagined you here, standing just so, inviting my love.'

After which revealing speech, he sat down on the bed, covering his face with his hands. The curtain over the open window moved in the draught, catching Jo's eye, and she recalled her errand with a gasp of dismay.

'Marc, you're in danger!' she cried urgently.

He looked up at her, his eyes alight.

'And so, *ma belle*, are you.'

'Marc, there's no time . . . he's out there . . . Jacques! I think he has a gun.'

'*Mon Dieu!*' Marcel sprang up from the bed, but as he moved towards the window, Jo leaped in front of him.

'No, don't, he might shoot!'

Marcel thrust her aside, reached the window, pulling aside the curtains, and looked out at the moonlit night. Jo covered her ears with her hands, expecting every moment to hear a report and to see Marcel fall.

'There is no one there,' he told her.

'But there was . . . I saw him.'

'Did you?' He turned to look at her, suspicion and disbelief plain in his expression; the chiselled features had hardened, his lips curling sardonically as he surveyed her désabillé. '*Vas t'en*, Jo, this is one prank too many.'

'It isn't a prank,' Jo declared insistently. 'He was standing under your window, and I ran to warn you without waiting to put anything on.'

'So I see.' He glanced away from her flimsy covering.

Jo was bewildered by the sudden change in him. He had been at her feet, an ardent lover, now he had become a cold, sarcastic admonisher. Had he really believed she was the embodiment of a fantasy? But he must have discovered when he embraced her that she was flesh and blood, or had he imagined she was someone else? Some woman who haunted his imagination as he did hers? Though originally she had had the wild idea of coming to him, she had rejected it, and she was entirely innocent of any ulterior motive. Her intent had been to save him from possible extinction, and his insinuations were wholly unjust. Conscious of outraged virtue, for she *had* resisted temptation, she crossed her arms over her bosom, and said indignantly:

'I know what you're thinking, Marc, but you're quite, quite wrong. I *did* see Jacques outside, and my only thought was to warn you in time.' Reminded of his danger, she frowned anxiously. 'He may still be outside lurking in the bushes, waiting until you've put your light out. Hadn't you better wake the servants and order them to search for him?'

'And have them laughing at me for being a nervous idiot? As if Jacques is capable of attempting murder!' He laughed scornfully. 'You must have been dreaming.'

He drew a quick breath, his nostrils expanding, while his eyes began to glitter.

'*Mon Dieu*, Jo, this is too much! There is a limit to my self-control.'

'Is there?' She smiled seductively. Fate had led her into the very situation she had contemplated and reluctantly dismissed as damaging to her self-respect and unfair to her father. Marcel had betrayed he was far from indifferent to her, and all other considerations faded from her mind. Child of the permissive age, she would not allow a few scruples to stand in their way, when she wanted him so desperately, and he wanted her.

'I love you, Marc,' she said simply, and saw him start. 'You want me, you can't go on pretending you don't.' He made as if to speak, but she rushed on impetuously, 'I know you're going to marry Yolande Latour, and you have a *bien-aimée* in Paris who is more attractive than I am, but they aren't here and I am.' Her eyes became luminous and she held out her arms to him. 'Love me tonight and I'll ask for nothing more.'

He made a movement towards her, his passion kindling in response, but stopped abruptly and turned towards the window.

'*Tu es folle*,' he muttered hoarsely.

'It's good to be a little mad sometimes,' Jo returned, disappointed that he had not accepted the invitation of her arms. 'You may recall that you said you'd teach me how to love—at least, that was what you implied. I hated you then, but you also said hate was akin to loving. You see, I have become an apt pupil, for you've woken me up, as you wanted to do.' She moved across the room and twined her arms about his neck, pressing herself against his bare back. 'You can't repudiate me now, after all you've said.'

She felt a tremor run through him.

'*Mon Dieu*, what have I done?' he murmured. Then he became rigid in her clasp.

'It will not do, Josephine,' he said, gently removing her clinging arms. 'Not like this. Your father entrusted you into my care, and I cannot betray his trust.'

At mention of her father, Jo drew back. Again she felt bewildered; Marcel's reaction was so unexpected.

'It's my life,' she said defiantly. 'I can do what I like with it.'

'Not with my contrivance.' He stiffened, peering down into the garden. 'There *is* something moving out there.'

Instantly Jo forgot everything but the menace outside. She stared out over his shoulder at the moonlight landscape.

'Marc, you must do something to protect yourself!'

'What, from that *canaille*? He has gone again.' He closed the window, drawing the curtains across it, and Jo wondered if he had really seen anything or had merely sought to divert her. He turned back to face her and now he had himself completely under control.

'*Ma chère petite fille*, your offer was very generous and I appreciate it, but I am not such a cad as to take advantage of it. In spite of the scent,' he smiled almost tenderly, his stern features softening, 'you are not a tart, and are far too innocent to know what you are doing. I have been at fault by putting ideas into your head, but . . .' he looked away from her, 'you can be so damned provocative, and that is my only excuse. You are very young and vulnerable, and I do not seduce virgins.'

Jo felt a scorching flame of humiliation licking at her deflated ego. Marcel was telling her she was too young and naïve to interest him seriously. All his amorous innuendoes, his kisses, had meant nothing. She told him:

'There has to be a first time, and I'd rather it was you than Terry.'

She had the satisfaction of seeing jealousy—could it be jealousy?—contort his face. He seized her by her shoulders, his hard fingers digging into the soft flesh beneath the thin nylon, and shook her violently.

'*Enfant du diable*,' he muttered savagely, 'will you drive me crazy?'

'Yes,' she returned coolly, 'I'd like to.'

But Marcel quickly controlled his passion. He released his hold of her, giving her a little push, and she was sure her shoulders would show bruises where he had gripped her. He said quietly:

'I refuse to give Grand'mère and Yo an excuse to throw mud at you.'

The reminder of Yolande was like a cold shower.

'I see, Miss Latour would be shocked to hear that I'd been in your room, even though I have a perfectly legitimate excuse.' Jo's voice rose shrilly. 'You're scared she might ditch you if she discovered what hasn't happened!'

'Hush!' He glanced towards the door. 'I will explain about Yo upon a more suitable occasion. There is a time and place for everything, and this is neither.'

He crossed the room and stared moodily at the photograph beside his bed as if his grandmother's face was reminding him of his duty. He said laconically:

'After the *bal masqué* I shall announce our engagement.'

Jo went cold. 'So soon?' she whispered.

Marcel gave her a comprehensive glance.

'High time, I should say.' He picked up his jacket and threw it at her. 'Put that round you, Jo, you are too damned enticing without a covering.'

'I wish I could entice you,' Jo murmured rebelliously as she slipped her arms into the jacket. It was lined with silk and smelt faintly of tobacco and after shave.

'Oh, Josephine—Jo!' Marcel was half laughing, half angry. 'Bullheaded, rash impetuous little madcap! When will you grow up?'

He took his robe off a hook on the bathroom door and put it on; it was a brocade affair in black and gold, which was very becoming.

'I am grown up,' Jo said sullenly, 'and I'd like to know what your lady in Paris has got that I haven't.'

'What lady in Paris?'

'Your mistress.'

'I have no mistress in Paris or anywhere else.'

'But you implied that you had when I asked you.'

'I am sure I did not, what I did say was that it was not a fit subject for *une jeune fille*.'

'You always treat me like a child,' Jo said wearily. 'That's the trouble, isn't it? You consider I'm too young for you.'

'Not at all—your youth, your eagerness for life, your honesty and candour are what I like about you.'

'Like but not love,' she said mournfully, sitting down on the edge of the bed.

'Take the chair, please, Jo,' he said harshly. 'The bed is too evocative.'

Meekly she obeyed, quelling a pert retort. Marcel had completely regained command of both himself and the situation. The enchanted moments in his arms might never have been. She ought to go back to her room, but she was loath to leave him, for there was still the possibility that Jacques was lurking outside, and the presence of another person might deter him if he were contemplating an assault.

'Those châteaux were so romantic,' she said dreamily, expecting dismissal and trying to keep him talking. 'All those lovely ladies Diane de Poitiers, Agnès Sorel, Madame Pompadour . . . their lovers weren't bothered with scruples.'

'I am not a king,' Marcel pointed out. 'They could not marry whom they chose, and their consorts were not always compatible.'

'No, but you're the Comte de Savigny, and also have obligations,' she returned tartly. She would insist upon returning home, she thought despondently; she could not bear to be present at the *bal masqué* and witness Yolande's triumph when Marcel announced their engagement.

'I am not—as I have repeatedly told you, the title is obsolete,' Marcel insisted. 'I am a breeder of horses and a farmer like your father, though it is true I do have obligations to the estate.'

'Which are more important than love.' For he could only retain the château with Yolande's money. He came to stand beside her, ignoring her remark, and started to stroke her head lightly.

'You have beautiful hair, Jo, the colour of autumn leaves, and it is soft as silk. You are still so young, in spite of your protestations, you believe that this love of yours, which I assure you is only the first awakening of your womanhood, should have instant satisfaction, a view held by most of your age group, but you need time to test your feelings before you do something irrevocable.'

Jo darted a swift glance up at him, her eyes stormy. His face was inscrutable, his downcast eyes concealed by his thick lashes. She jerked her head away, unable any longer to endure his light caress, which was what he would use to soothe a fractious child. He had rejected her and was trying to soften his rejection with a lot of meaningless words. He would do nothing to jeopardise his standing with Yolande whom he meant to make his wife.

'I shall tell Thérèse our engagement is off,' she said decidedly. 'That I've found I couldn't endure life here at Savigny. Luckily you left me that loophole, which I'm sure you expected me to take.'

'Why did you say we were engaged in the first place, Jo?' he asked negligently, though there was suppressed eagerness in his eyes, which she did not perceive, her gaze being fixed upon her hands clasped in her lap.

She shrugged her shoulders. 'As I said before, it was just a sick joke . . . that misfired.'

'Yes, you have rather a misplaced sense of humour, but at least it gave me the opportunity to claim a few kisses.'

'Oh, for heaven's sake!' Jo sprang to her feet. 'You won't get any more.'

Those kisses had meant something to her, though he had accepted them so lightly.

'Opportunities or kisses?' he asked, grinning.

'Both.'

'Yet you are still here in my room,' he reminded her pointedly. He moved restlessly. 'Might I suggest you go back to your own? I am only human, Jo.'

He was weakening, but she no longer desired him to make love to her; she was too deeply wounded by his careless dismissal of her love, as if she did not know the depth of her own feelings much better than he could, and the imminence of his engagement to Yolande. He was a callous, cynical brute, she told herself angrily, and why she cared for him so deeply was a mystery. Right from the beginning he had used her as a diversion, amused himself by arousing her and teasing her. But he baulked at going all the way, because that might commit him more deeply than he wished to become. Nor did she fully credit that the Parisian mistress was a myth. There must be a woman somewhere in his life; he was no ascetic and he was a Frenchman. She had seen enough to know Yolande did not attract him sexually, he was marrying her for convenience, and it might be there was a vacancy in his love life at that moment, but he considered she was too young and inexperienced to fill it. That was the sum total of all he had been saying. But she would not be available for any more erotic passages when he was feeling bored. She drew herself up proudly, the light making a flaming nimbus of her hair, ruffled by his fingers, her eyes wide and scornful.

'I'm going,' she said disdainfully. 'I've no wish to further strain your ... er ... humanity, if that's what you call it. I could use a less pretty word.' He took a step towards her and she retreated hastily before the sudden fire in his eyes. 'I apologise for my intrusion,' she went on, 'it was well meant. I *did* see someone on the terrace, and I thought he intended to take a pot shot at you, but you're too vain to believe me. You thought I'd succumbed to your masculine charm, which was not the case. If I've teased you, by being provocative, it was in return for the many times you've teased me, but I never had the slightest intention of going to bed with you.'

Pride demanded that he should believe her, but that seemed doubtful, for he said softly:

'Did you not, Jo?'

'No, and I meant what I said about telling Thérèse our engagement was off. I want to end all intimate connections with you here and now.'

Marcel's mouth thinned to a hard line.

'You will tell my sister nothing of the sort.'

She shook her head defiantly and moved towards the door, but he stepped between her and it, his fingers on the handle, a dark-robed, tall, menacing figure.

'From henceforth I shall call the tune and you will do as I say. Unless you want me to tell her the truth, that it was a stupid joke on your part and I supported it to save your face.'

Jo drew back, her face flushing. She did not want Thérèse to learn that she had been the victim of a hoax, she would be hurt. Marcel was showing himself as she had first assessed him, tyrannical, arrogant and unfeeling.

'Cynical devil!' she muttered.

'Call me what you like if it relieves your feelings,' he returned imperturbably, 'but please understand our engagement still stands until I myself choose to explain to Thérèse.'

He opened the door, and peered into the dark passage.

'You may go now, the way is clear. Goodnight.'

Jo took off his jacket and threw it at him.

'That's too incriminating to take to my room,' she said loftily, and swept past him, her head held high, blinking back tears that threatened to fall. He caught her round the waist before she had crossed the threshold, his arm like a steel trap about her body, and imprinted a burning kiss on the space below her ear.

'Goodnight, sweet termagant,' he murmured. Unpredictable man, his eyes were alight with merriment as if he found her attempt at a dignified exit funny. *Dors bien.'*

Jo resisted an impulse to slap his face, but that sort of retaliation would only provoke him to some sort of violent reaction and she was too spent and weary for any further exchange. The long day at Chenonceaux and the subsequent emotional turmoil had caught up with her. Marcel held the door open to light the passage as she stumbled towards her room. He would not risk turning on the passage switch. He stood watching her retreat, until she had entered her room, but she did not look back.

Arrived there, she made a grimace at her father's photograph.

'It's all right, Daddy,' she addressed it aloud. 'I'm still virgo intacta, but it's more by good luck than good management.'

Then she threw herself on her bed in a storm of tears.

CHAPTER NINE

EXHAUSTED though she was, Jo only slept fitfully, and awoke in a cold sweat from a dream in which Jacques was hunting Marcel through a forest and she was powerless to warn him. It was still dark, but further sleep eluded her, and the atmosphere of the room seemed close and oppressive. She got up and looked out of the window to see the sky was beginning to lighten. She had a great longing to be out of doors, so she showered and dressed in slacks and a thin sweater, then crept downstairs, lighting her way with a pocket torch. The massive bolts on the front door were intimidating, but they were kept well oiled, and slid back when she exerted all her strength. The Château de Savigny, like many others, had originally been designed to be a fortress, but the iron-bound door was all that was left of the former building. Jo stepped out on to the terrace and looked back at it. No light showed anywhere, and it looked grim and menacing against the now grey sky.

Instinctively she turned her steps towards the stables, which were familiar territory. She was resolving that somehow she must persuade her father to allow her to return home. If he realised how unhappy she was, she was sure he would recall her. She would find an opportunity to telephone him without eavesdroppers, and one hint that Marcel was not what he believed him to be would do the trick. That she might be maligning her host did not trouble her; Marcel did not deserve any consideration from her and surely he would be glad to be rid of her after the embarrassment she had caused him. She must, she simply *must* leave the château before the *bal masqué* and the announcement of Marcel's engagement to Yolande Latour.

It was still too early for the stable staff to be at work. She decided she would saddle the palomino mare herself and go for a morning ride, though she was not supposed to go out on her own. She was not afraid of encountering Jacques; he had no quarrel with her, and he had always been friendly towards her. He was the man who had come to fetch Lucifer from Greyfriars, and their kindred interest in the stallion had been a bond between them.

There was no lock on the gate into the yard, but as she pushed it open, the Doberman guard dog came growling towards her. He knew her, and as soon as he recognised her, started to wag his stump of a tail in friendly greeting. She had been reprimanded for making a fuss of him.

'Guard dogs are useless if made into pets,' Marcel had told her severely, but Jo had ignored his dictum when he was not there, and now her overtures were paying off.

There were rooms in the main building, formerly the coach-house, which was adorned with a small tower and a clock. Two of the stable lads slept there in turns and were supposed to keep an eye on the premises, but they relied upon the Doberman to wake them if any intruder came into the yard. The clock showed it was not yet five o'clock, and the light had brightened. As Jo reached up to lift her saddle off its peg, she heard a slight sound, and the dog which had followed her went back into the yard. Her heart quickened its beat as it occurred to her that Marcel might have had the same idea as herself. Abandoning the saddle, she went to the door and peered cautiously round it. Jacques was walking stealthily towards Lucifer's box, and the light glinted on the weapon he held, not a gun but a wicked-looking knife. Intuition told her what his object was; he had baulked at attacking Marcel, and now his vengeance was directed towards his ex-master's most prized possession. His hatred of the man was greater than his affection for the horse, and to maim an animal was not a capital offence even if it were traced to him. He was already unlatching the door, as Jo ran towards him. He had disappeared inside when she reached it, and she rushed in after him with no thought of danger to herself. Lucifer recognised his groom, as the Doberman had also done, and turned his head, nickering softly, expecting his morning feed. Jacques made a lunge for his back tendons, but Jo had caught his arm. She fought to wrest the knife from him, but for all his small size, Jacques was strong and wiry, she shouted desperately:

'Help! *Aidez moi! Au secours!*'

The Doberman began to bark.

Uttering a stream of invective, Jacques threw Jo off, and advanced upon her, his knife raised, the light of madness in his eyes. But before he reached her shrinking figure, he was struck down. Lucifer was not tied to his manger, and alarmed by the commotion behind him had swung round. Jo caught a glimpse of him as he reared, ears flat, eyes rolling, teeth bared, his front hoofs flailing. One of them sent the little man sprawling. Jo made for the open door, hoping to escape before he recovered, slipped on some fouled straw and fell, catching her head on the lock of the door, which was swinging shut under the frenzied onslaught of the Doberman. She knew no more.

She returned to consciousness and a medley of confused impressions. She was lying on her bed in her room in the château, but at first she thought it was at Greyfriars. Her head ached, her throat was sore, and she was burning hot, drawing her breath with difficulty. A woman in a dark dress and white headdress came and went.

'Daddy,' Jo muttered, 'I want Daddy.'

But all that came was a strange monster with one huge eye in a dark frame, which hauled her into sitting position and made her senses reel. Then it vanished together with the strange woman, and Marcel was there.

He bent over her and his voice was thick with emotion.

'*Mon ange, ma chérie*, speak to me!'

She was not his angel, or his darling, he had repulsed her, why must he torment her with love words?

'Go away, mocking devil!' she shouted at him—at least she thought she shouted, but her voice was low and hoarse.

Then all was confusion again, Lucifer's rearing form, Jacques' menacing face, until mercifully she slept, and dreamed. But now it was Marcel she saw, Marcel in black brocade ordering her from his room.

'But I thought you loved me,' she sobbed in her dream.

She saw his cynical smile, his contemptuous air.

'Love is nothing but a biological urge, and I need Yo's money. I am going to marry her.'

Yolande with a triumphant expression, her green eyes peering over Marcel's shoulders. The images came and went.

On the second morning after her accident, Jo woke to recognise the white-capped woman seated beside her. So she was real, not an illusion. She had a calm sweet face and was a nursing Sister.

'I have been ill?' Jo asked her.

'*Comment?*'

Jo tried again. '*Je suis malade?*'

The nun understood that. '*Une fièvre*', she said, 'But now he go. You better soon.'

But the visions returned. Jo tossed and muttered. The Sister gave her an opiate.

The following morning she really was better, the fever had left her and she felt weak, but cool. This time she found her father seated beside her.

'Oh, Daddy!' She clutched at him, fearful that he too was a phantom created by her distraught imagination. 'You'll take me home?'

'When you're strong enough, dear.' He took her hands in his. 'My poor darling, you've had a bad time.'

'Awful,' she sighed, but she was thinking of Marcel, not of her illness. 'How did you get here?'

'I was sent for when you were hurt.'

'And you won't disappear?'

'Disappear?' He grinned and pressed her hands. 'Did you think I was a ghost? Aren't my fingers substantial enough?'

'There've been so many of them,' she told him. 'They come and go. Marcel came, Miss Latour, Lucifer . . .'

'You've been delirious, darling. You had a blow on the head, followed by pneumonia. But antibiotics have got your temperature down. Marcel was afraid your skull might be fractured. He arranged for X-ray apparatus to be brought here so you need not be moved, and engaged Sister Véronique to nurse you. Luckily there was no break, and you'll be no crazier than you always were.'

'I must have been an awful nuisance,' Jo said slowly. 'Why wasn't I sent to hospital?'

'Marcel wouldn't hear of it,' Roger explained. 'Thought the journey would be too trying for you, or so I was told. He spoke to me on the phone, and since we haven't started harvest I was able to come at once. But you've talked enough for now, darling. You mustn't tire yourself.'

There were many questions Jo wanted to ask, but she was very weak. Marcel apparently had been very generous and very kind. As far as she knew he had not been to see her—he probably thought it better not to appear personally interested in her after all that had occurred. Yolande might be suspicious, though she did not know of that midnight scene in his bedroom, the memory of which still seared her. Perhaps Marcel would tell her about it when they were married; married people should not have secrets from each other. He would tell her how he had had to deal with a lovesick adolescent and would make it all sound very humorous. But by that time she would be safely home again and all that had happened in France would seem like a dream; a lot of it seemed dreamlike even now, mixed up with the fantasies that had beset her during her fever.

On the next day Thérèse was permitted to come to see her and complained bitterly about her banishment from the sick room.

'That Sister of Mercy told me I was too vital, too lively, and I would disturb you with my chatter. As if I would! She takes too much upon herself, but you are really better, *chérie*, I do not disturb you?'

'No, you cheer me up.' Jo was smiling. She hesitated. 'Is your brother at home?'

'Marc? No, he is in Paris.' Jo flinched. Had he gone to the mistress whom he had declared did not exist? Having a last fling before proposing to Yolande?

Thérèse was looking at her wonderingly.

'It is most strange,' she said. 'He came to see you when you were ill, and you became very agitated and called him a devil. So he did not come again.'

Mocking devil, she had called him, but that was before she had been ill.

'I was off my head,' she reminded Thérèse. 'Didn't he realise that?'

Thérèse pleated the coverlet with nervous fingers.

'You had to be kept quiet, but I would have thought . . .' she broke off.

'That Marc was the one person I would want near me,' Jo finished her sentence, for Thérèse believed they were in love. The care and expense Marc had lavished upon her would support that misconception, but perhaps he had felt some responsibility for her condition. Her feelings were unchanged, but he would be relieved to be quit of her. She went on with an effort:

'The truth is we had a row just before this happened.' She touched her head. 'I suppose that's what I remembered.'

Thérèse did not look satisfied, and Jo changed the subject.

'What has happened about the *bal masqué*? Is it still on?'

'Oh, but of course, and we hope very much you will be strong enough to attend it, at any rate for a little while.'

'That's nice of you, but I shall be going home.'

'Ah, no, that you cannot do. You must be here on my birthday or it will all be spoiled. It was to be for you too, remember?'

'Yes, I remember,' Jo said faintly. Marcel had insisted upon that so long ago when first she had come to the château. He would not insist now, unless he wanted to wreak a subtle revenge by forcing her to hear the announcement of his engagement to Yolande.

'Besides,' Thérèse went on with a puzzled frown, 'you are betrothed to Marc.'

'Not any more,' Jo said hardly. 'That was what the row was about. I . . . I had to tell him I couldn't bear to live at the château.'

'*Ah, bon?*' Thérèse looked distressed. 'But Jo, *chérie*, Marc will not always live here. He plans to move to one of his farms, and that would suit you, being a farmer's daughter.'

Jo shook her head. 'He's given that idea up, he'll never leave the château.' For wasn't he marrying Yolande to have the means to restore it?

'But, *chérie*——' Thérèse began, then noticing the signs of strain in Jo's white face, went on, 'We must not talk about it any more, if it distresses you. As you know, your papa is staying here.' She giggled. 'He has been a great success with Grand'mère, he plays up to her and she adores it.'

'Perhaps that will reconcile her to having an invalid foisted upon her,' Jo said sourly, for she was sure Madame de Savigny must resent her illness, 'but I hope it won't be for much longer.'

'You must not talk so,' Thérèse reproved her. 'Grand'-mère is not a monster. She thinks you were very brave . . .'

At that point Sister Véronique came in and ordered Thérèse out. Her patient must rest. Jo was not sorry for the interruption; much as she liked Thérèse, there were so many subjects that were painful to discuss with her. At least she had disposed of her mock engagement; she was thankful to have finished with that. Marcel had told her to leave it to him to tell Thérèse, but he had not done so, and she could not keep up the deception any longer. From Thérèse her thoughts went back to that morning in the stable; she was still very vague about what had occurred. Jacques—had he been hurt? And Lucifer ... Her last recollection was of the great horse on his hind legs pawing the air. She did not think Jacques had touched him, but were either her father or Thérèse cognisant of the facts?

Next morning she was allowed to sit up in a chair by the window and was surprised to discover how wobbly her legs were. Sister Véronique assured her they would soon regain their strength, she was young, and youth was resilient.

So at last there's some advantage in being young, Jo thought wryly. She had glanced at herself in the mirror as she moved to the chair. Her dressing gown was a serviceable woollen affair with a tie belt, and it seemed to hang on her. Could one lose so much weight in so short a period? for she had not been ill very long. Her face was very white, her eyes enormous, and her hair all the redder in contrast. I look hideous, she thought despondently.

Her father came in and said how glad he was to see her up, and she smiled wanly.

'I'm pining for the good air of Greyfriars to complete my cure.'

He looked at her curiously. 'I find the air here very pleasant.'

'Perhaps I've never become fully acclimatised to it. But how is Luci? He wasn't hurt, was he?'

'Oh no, *he* wasn't. He's fine.' Roger looked uncomfortable, and, always intuitive where her affections were concerned, Jo demanded:

'Something is wrong, isn't it? Tell me, did he ... kill Jacques?'

Her father nodded. 'You'll have to know some time. There was an inquest, of course, and the coroner, while returning a verdict of accidental death, recommended that Lucifer should be destroyed.'

'Oh no!' Jo was horrified. 'That's not fair! Jacques had a knife, he meant to hamstring him.' Full recollection was returning to her. 'He was wild with Marc for dismissing him, and sought a cowardly revenge. I think he was very drunk. When I tried to stop him, he turned on me.'

She shuddered and covered her face with her hands, recalling that dreadful moment.

'I didn't know that,' her father told her. 'Marcel said he found you by the stable door and carried you in.'

Sister Véronique came in followed by Louise carrying a tray of coffee. She looked at Jo, and tartly told Roger to go, but Jo was herself again.

'No, he's staying,' she said firmly. 'We have things to do. We must tell the true story to save Lucifer before it's too late.' She turned to her father. 'Is Marc in Paris?'

'Yes, dealing with the litigation regarding Jacques Dubois' death. But didn't Lucifer strike you too?'

'Oh no, I was trying to get out and fell, catching my head on something on the door.'

'All the same, I'm afraid the coroner regarded Lucifer as a dangerous animal, though Marcel has appealed on his behalf.'

'But it was an accident Luci was scared, he didn't mean to kill. He's not used to people fighting in his box and I'm sure he knew Jacques meant to harm me.' Jo half rose from her chair. 'I must go to Paris to defend him. Why should a noble animal be destroyed because he struck a little rat who was trying to injure him?'

Colour had risen in her cheeks and her eyes were sparkling at the prospect of conflict, and Sister Véronique glanced at her uneasily.

'Your temperature is rising,' she warned in her accented English.

'Oh, rot!' Jo ejaculated with all her old vigour. 'Daddy, you must get in touch with Marc and make sure he knows the true facts. You see, only I know exactly what happened before I was knocked out, and I've been so vague and stupid with being ill and all that.' Her expression became anxious. 'Luci is all right, he's still here?'

'Yes, he's here.' Roger's eyes twinkled. 'Lucifer's predicament will effect a complete cure, I'm sure. Don't you worry, Sister, I know our Jo, she's a lot tougher than you think, and she always was a firebrand where anything she loved was concerned.'

Jo sank back in her chair. Anything she loved—but Marcel whom she loved most of all had had nothing from her but a blow in the face and the rough edge of her tongue. She had always been ready to misjudge him. When Thérèse had told her he had gone to Paris, she had immediately surmised that it was to see a woman, when he was fighting to save the fine animal they both loved.

'Give me a cup of coffee, please,' she said to Louise, who was hovering near the door. Then to her nurse, 'Don't worry about me. I'm not running a temperature, in fact I feel stronger every minute. Action is a tonic, you know.'

Louise handed Jo the coffee, and poured more for Roger and Sister Véronique, who was making a vain effort to feel Jo's pulse. Louise was glad to be ministering to the English miss again, whom she had always admired. Over the rim of her cup, Jo looked fixedly at her father as she insisted:

'You will get in touch with Marc, Daddy, as soon as ever you can? I shan't rest until you do.'

Again Roger looked troubled. 'Marcel won't want you to be involved. You couldn't be called as a witness because you were ill, and the coroner considered it was a clear case of a stallion savaging a groom and no further testimony was needed.'

'But that's ridiculous!' Jo half rose from her chair. 'I'm the witness for the defence, as it were. If Marc is being stupid you must inform the police of the true facts, or I'll do it myself.'

'Oh, you'd better leave it to me,' her father said hastily. He knew Marcel would hate Jo's name to appear in the papers, but if she were thwarted she was capable of some crazy action.

A *gendarme* came to take Jo's statement and he agreed that Jacques' attack upon herself altered the situation, but he was not sanguine about Lucifer's fate. Whether it was an accident or not, a man had died.

But no one had anticipated the reaction of the press. Scenting a story, reporters and photographers arrived at the château. Brushing Gaston aside as he tried to turn them away, Jo went out to them, realising publicity might help Lucifer's cause.

They photographed Lucifer, the stable yard, the château, and Jo herself feeding the horse with sugar lumps to emphasise his gentleness. She was in mortal terror that the animal would take exception to the cameras, but to her relief he behaved beautifully. The newspapermen retired with their booty, after paying Jo fulsome compliments and assuring her that they would arouse public opinion on Lucifer's behalf.

In due course, the photographs appeared in the papers, with articles praising Josephine Thornton's heroic action. She was likened to Joan of Arc, and Lucifer was the hero who had saved her from a drunken man's attack.

Unfortunately the de Savigny's were disgusted, as they considered newspaper reportage the height of vulgarity. Solange was livid, the older servants shocked, and even Thérèse enquired if it had been necessary. Jo was in disgrace, but public opinion had won a reprieve for Lucifer, which was all that mattered to her.

She had her father's presence to support her in that chilly atmosphere, but even Roger seemed a little stunned by the furore Jo's disclosures had evoked. He remarked dourly that other news must be short, or else the public were glad of a diversion from strikes and bankruptcies.

'You and Lucifer are very photogenic,' he told Jo with a twinkle. 'And Frenchmen always appreciate a pretty woman. You'll be having a film offer next.'

'God forbid!' Jo exclaimed fervently.

Throughout the proceedings there had been no word from the master of the château himself, and Roger was apprehensive about that, though he concealed his anxiety from his daughter. Having arrived at a very satisfactory arrangement with Marcel he did not want it to be disrupted by Jo's rash conduct. She was leading a normal life again and had ventured out on her palomino mare, and was relieved to notice Lucifer had been transferred to another box.

When they were all assembled for lunch, some three days later, Thérèse started to complain about her brother's absence. He was needed to organise the preparations for her birthday.

'I cannot think what can be keeping him,' she said.

'Can you not?' Solange de Savigny fixed Jo with a basilisk stare. 'He cannot appreciate the notoriety that our heroic guest has brought upon us' she said sourly. 'He must have found all that publicity most obnoxious.'

Jo restrained a retort that it was a small price to pay for Lucifer's life, for Madame cared little for animals and would take the opposite point of view. She hoped she had not offended Marcel; surely he would be more understanding?

Thérèse said, 'All the more reason to retire here, it must be worse in Paris.'

'That is not so,' Solange told here. 'Paris is large, a man can lose himself there, but here we are vulnerable. Do you know Gaston had to order a coachload of sightseers off the premises yesterday? The *canaille* wanted to view the stables as part of their tour of the châteaux.'

'It's a mercy they didn't get to them,' Roger remarked. 'They might have found Lucifer was far from the gentle lamb he's been represented to be.'

'It's just a nine days' wonder,' Jo sought to soothe them. 'It'll soon be forgotten and I shall have gone. Daddy is needed on the farm and I shall return with him.'

'But our *fête* day!' Therese wailed. 'You must stay for that.'

'Oh, except for you, dear, I shan't be missed,' Jo said firmly.

Roger and Madame de Savigny exchanged glances, and Roger cleared his throat. 'You'll have to wait to see Marcel about that,' he told Jo, giving her an enigmatic look.

'Well, naturally I want to thank him for all his trouble.' Jo's colour had risen. 'But I could always write to him.'

She did not want to be present at the masked ball.

But that proved to be unnecessary, because that night Marcel came home. He had neither telephoned nor written, so his arrival was unheralded. Jo encountered him in the hall on her way to go upstairs to dress for dinner. She was much thinner and paler than when he had last seen her, with a fragile look about her instead of her normal healthy bloom.

She paused with her foot on the first step as he called her name, while her heart began to beat wildly. With an effort she turned to face him.

'Monsieur de Savigny, this is a surprise—I didn't know you were expected.'

'What formality!' he exclaimed mockingly. 'What has happened to Marc?'

'Oh, he ceased to exist as far as I'm concerned when you showed me the door.' She strove to speak lightly and forced a laugh. 'I must apologise for all the fireworks I seem to have caused in Paris, but I had to save Luci.'

'*Bien entendu*, but you, *ma chère*, are you fully recovered? You are very pale.'

'Which means I must be looking horribly plain.'

'You could never look plain to me.'

She moved her shoulders. 'Don't you know by now that I don't appreciate French gallantry?' She had been looking anywhere but at him. The memory of that night in his room when he had misconstrued the reason for her coming still scorched her when she remembered it, and his reappearance had recalled it vividly. Then, recollecting how much she owed him for the nursing and attention she had received, she forced herself to meet his eyes and said more graciously:

'I'm glad to have this opportunity to thank you for the care you've had lavished on me, but you should have sent me to hospital.'

Marc came up to her and laid his hand over hers that rested on the banister, preventing the flight she was contemplating.

'This last prank of yours was a little expensive,' he

said drily. 'What on earth were you doing in the stables at dawn?'

'Restoring my battered ego with the only companions I really care about,' she returned frankly, 'and if I hadn't gone there, Lucifer would have been hopelessly lamed.'

His face darkened and his hand clenched over hers.

'That despicable rat! He deserved what he got.'

'My sentiments exactly.' She wondered if she dared enquire if he now realised her fears about Jacques were justified, and that she had come to him with a genuine warning, but decided it was better not to reopen the subject. She went on:

'But I didn't want Luci to be branded as a killer, so please forgive me for all the hoo-ha in the press which has exceedingly offended your good grandmother.'

She spoke at random, aware in every quivering nerve of his hand over hers on the banister. She had tried hard to stifle her love for him, concentrating upon her return to Greyfriars, though she had longed to see him again, yet half hoping she would be spared the ordeal. Now he was here, touching her, emotion was surging within her. She yearned to throw herself into his arms, to feel his lips on hers, the hard pressure of his embrace, but she must remind herself that it had only been a game to him, and any weakness on her part would only damage her pride further. She tried to withdraw her hand, but he held it firmly.

As he did not speak, she went on desperately,

'I'm sure your family will want to greet you, and I'll be late for dinner if I don't go and change.'

He raised his brows. 'I am dismissed?'

'Well . . . er . . . Oh, what do you want of me, Marc? Everything is over between us—not that there ever was much.'

He reached for her other hand, and holding both in his, told her:

'I insisted upon seeing you when you were feverish, but you did not know me, or I hope you did not, for you called me a devil.'

'So Thérèse said.'

'Oh, did she? She was always indiscreet.'

'I ... I was off my head, Marc, I didn't mean it.'

'I am glad to hear that.'

'But you ... went away.'

'Reluctantly, but when I found my presence only agitated you, there was no point in staying and I had much to do in Paris in connection with Jacques' death. Perhaps I had been too harsh with him, but I cannot tolerate negligence. Anyway, he would have drunk himself to death, so perhaps his end was a merciful deliverance.'

'He brought it on himself, so there's no blame attached to you,' Jo assured him. Standing on the step above him, her face was level with his, and she saw there were lines about his eyes and mouth and a look of strain. Evidently he had been through a difficult time, and she continued gently:

'You look tired, Marc, but it's all over now, and since you're home again, you can rest.'

'With Thérèse's *bal masqué* to organise?'

'Can't she do it herself?' Jo felt a stab, for it was not only Thérèse's *fête*, but his own approaching engagement for which he would be preparing. There would be bound to be a stir in the neighbourhood when that was announced, many relatives and friends calling to congratulate him, for though he had only a small immediate family, there were many distant connections of the de Savignys who would want to pay their respects. 'Please let me go, Marc,' she pleaded, trying to free her hands. 'I really must go and change.'

'Running away?' There was a glint in his eyes.

'No, why should I? Marc . . .'

Then Thérèse came out into the gallery, already changed, and seeing her brother, came tearing down the stairs to hurl herself at Marcel.

'At last! *Mon cher frère!*'

Marcel loosed Jo's hands during her precipitous descent, and opened his arms to receive her. Jo beat a hasty retreat up the stairs, hoping that Thérèse had not come to a wrong conclusion from the attitude in which she had surprised them.

CHAPTER TEN

To Jo's dismay her father yielded to the de Savignys' pressing invitation to stay until after the masked ball. When she remonstrated, pointing out that he would be needed on the farm, he declared that he could be spared to take a holiday, as harvest had not yet begun and he had left a reliable man in charge. August was the harvest month and they were still in July.

'And surely you don't want to miss it?' he asked, looking at her with a slightly puzzled air. 'I can understand your wish to return with me, as you say you don't feel equal to the journey alone, and your very natural wish to be with your mother in the circumstances, but I'm given to understand this occasion has a special significance for you.'

It had, but he could not know that, and it was her turn to be mystified. But when she asked him to elucidate, he only looked knowing, remarking that he was neither blind nor stupid about what was going on, but he wasn't going to put his foot in it with any premature disclosures. He had a subtle air of conspiracy about him which baffled Jo, for he was a forthright man and it was unlike him to have a secret from her—besides, what was there to conceal? She had made a swift recovery, though she still looked a little frail, her indisposition and the Lucifer episode having occupied less than a fortnight, though it seemed to her very much longer. She could not tell her father that her anxiety to be gone was to avoid the announcement of Marcel's engagement to

Yolande, and she had managed to hide from him her emotional involvement—if it could be called that when it was so one-sided—with the master of Savigny. Though she was occasionally tempted to tell him the whole sad story, it would be better to keep her confidences until they had gone home and not while he was Marcel's guest. So she had no option but to acquiesce and steel herself to meet the coming ordeal with what fortitude she could muster.

Her father spent a lot of time with Marcel at one of his farms, which was some distance away on the banks of the Loir—not to be confused with the Loire, of which it was a tributary. Marcel was planning to transfer his horse breeding activities there, as there was better grazing than round the château. Thérèse told Jo there was an old manor house on the property which was being renovated, a charming old place, and she thought Marcel had some idea of living there if he had to sell the château, which he would not have to do if he married Yolande, she ended with a sigh, and reproachful look at Jo for breaking her engagement. Jo, of course, had never told her the true story of that.

Thérèse's birthday was during the last week of the month, only two days separating it from Jo's. Marcel was determined to do honour to the occasion, which was to be not only his sister's day, but to introduce the future mistress of Savigny. The district was still sufficiently feudal for that to be important, or so it seemed to Jo. Actually she had not seen Yolande since the accident, but as Marcel was always out, she concluded he was spending his time at St Pierre when he was not with her father. Workmen meanwhile were busy in the château. Coloured lights were festooned over its façade and outlined the towers, also outlining the approach as far as the gateway. The great entrance hall, normally so chilly and forbidding, was filled with banks of flowers. The huge dining table was extended to its full length, and would be loaded with provisions for a buffet supper. The carpet in the *salon* was removed and the floor waxed and polished for dancing. An air of festivity hung over the place as armies of cleaners, electricians and caterers swarmed through its precincts making their preparations.

Roger had scorned Jo's simple muslin dress.

'My daughter shall look as fine as any of these decadent toffs,' he had told her proudly, but fortunately when they were alone. He hired a gown from Paris for her from a theatrical costumiers. It was of cream silk, with an embroidered skirt and hem, with the puffed sleeves, low décolletage and high waist of the Empire period. The costume included a spangled scarf to be worn, not over her shoulders, but precariously draped over either arm, which was the way the Empire ladies wore them. Louise experimented with her hair, curling the heavy locks and dressing them high on her head with the addition of a switch of the same colour which she had procured with some difficulty. Jo had to admit the result was very becoming and added style to her costume. Jewels she had none, except her silver cross and chain, and Louise bemoaned the lack of a necklace, suggesting Madame de Savigny might be asked for the loan of one, but that Jo refused to consider. She knew the old woman's hostility had been increased by the publicity over Lucifer, and she was the last person of whom she could request a favour.

On the evening before the ball, Jo was on her way to bed, earlier than usual since she would need all her strength on the morrow, when Marcel came out of the dining room and called to her.

'One moment, Jo!'

She was surprised to see him. He had not been in to dinner; presumably he had been at St Pierre. Thérèse had declared that Yolande would not come to Savigny while Jo was there because she did not want to be contaminated by the presence of someone who had been mixed up in what she described as 'that deplorable affair', and had been greatly put out when she learned that the offender would be present at the ball. How true that was, Jo did not know, but she derived a dreary sort of satisfaction from the fact that Mademoiselle Latour would have to put up with it, albeit for the last time.

As Marcel came up to her, Jo experienced the familiar stir of her senses, and quickened pulse. He looked so very handsome and debonair in his frilled white shirt and velvet jacket. He thrust an oblong case into her hand.

'A little souvenir from me for saving Lucifer,' he told her with a wry smile.

'Thank you, but I didn't do it for reward.'

'I know that, but you deserve something. It is also your birthday present.'

Jo opened the case; it contained a necklace of glittering stones and a pair of ear-rings to match. They looked like diamonds, but surely they could not be.

'Are they real?' she asked stupidly.

Marcel drew himself up haughtily. 'Naturally, *ma mie*. Would I insult you with paste?'

Jo shut the case. 'I can't accept anything so valuable,' she protested.

'Lucifer is very valuable to me, and your father approves of the gift, so you need not scruple to accept it.'

'Oh, does he?' Jo wondered if Roger had any idea of what they must be worth. 'Thank you very much, Marcel, but would Mademoiselle Latour approve?'

'Definitely not, but her approval does not signify.' His lips twitched. 'Propriety does not become you, Jo, and for an amateur adventuress you are singularly un-enterprising. Have you not been told diamonds are a girl's best friend?'

Jo flushed, recalling her past follies, which seemed very childish now. Had she really aspired to be an ad-venturess? If so she had lamentably fallen down on the job. She would have played that scene in his bedroom very differently if her motives had been mercenary. Marcel was watching her with his normal quizzical expression and something else in his eyes.

'Take them, Jo,' he said softly. 'You have earned them, honourably.'

Jo summoned her courage to put the question she had not previously dared to ask, but which had troubled her ever since that night.

'So you know now that my fears about Jacques were not a fantasy? He *was* hanging about the grounds that night with evil intent, and I *did* see him and ran to warn you?'

Again his lips twitched. 'Yes, I realise your presence was perfectly legitimate, I feared it was too good to be true that you had come to offer yourself to me.'

Jo turned away her head, while the shamed blood flooded her cheeks. Mercifully he did not know that she nearly had.

'I would be grateful if you would forget all that. I didn't behave very well, but then neither did you.'

That one moment of crazy rapture when they had fused together oblivious of all else, but he had thought she was an hallucination, though why she should have so affected him she had never fathomed.

Marcel was shaking his dark head.

'I cannot do that. It is one of my most treasured memories.'

'I'm surprised to hear you say that. I hope you don't often have such ... such fantasies. Mademoiselle Latour won't appreciate them.'

'What has Yo to do with it?' he queried. 'You seem obsessed by her.'

'She looms rather large upon the horizon,' Jo said drily.

His long lashes descended over his eyes, which held a malicious gleam.

'I might almost surmise that you are jealous.' There was almost a purr in his voice, as if her possible jealousy pleased him.

'Of course I'm not,' Jo lied bravely.

'Again you disappoint me.'

'Oh, stop fooling!' Jo's exasperation sounded in her voice. He was deliberately tormenting her, for he knew she was not indifferent to him. She drew herself up proudly.

'I'll wear your diamonds, Marcel, as part of my costume, but afterwards I must return them. I neither deserve nor desire such a gift from you.'

'That is unreasonable.'

She shook her head.

'No, Marcel, at last I'm learning wisdom. Besides, I'd have no occasion to wear them at Greyfriars, and it would spoil their brilliance to keep them always in the bank.'

'*If* you return to Greyfriars.'

'Oh yes, I'm going, as soon as the ball is over.'

'*Qui vivra verra*,' he drawled.

'Oh, you'll live to see it,' she said tartly. 'Oh, I'm not ungrateful for your ... er ... hospitality, and you once said a visit to France would enlarge my horizons. It's done that. I've ... learned quite a lot. Au revoir, Marcel.'

She ran upstairs, but when she reached the gallery some impulse prompted her to look down. He was still standing where she had left him, watching her ascent, but his expression was neither sardonic nor mocking, a little tender smile was on his lips. Tender? Marcel? She was having delusions now. When had Marcel ever been tender towards her?

The evening of the ball was fine and warm, though there was no moon. Marcel, Madame de Savigny and Thérèse, since it was her celebration, stood at the foot of the stairs to receive the guests. Madame had stayed up for this auspicious occasion and was regal in black velvet and pearls. Her dresses always had a period look, so she was quite in the picture. Thérèse had chosen to represent Marguerite Gautier, the Dame aux Camélias, and was identifiable by the blossoms on her corsage and in her hair. She wore a hooped skirt, and her unruly hair was disciplined into the correct style. She carried her mask, which she would put on later, although it was hardly a disguise, and hoped to use it as cover for a little harmless flirtation. Marcel was a gentleman of the Empire in a beautifully tailored black velvet coat, double-breasted, cutaway and swallow-tailed. Under it he wore a black and silver vest, and a white silk cravat, completing his costume with tight white trousers and black half-boots. He had never looked more imposing and elegant. He had refused to powder his hair, but his own black locks had been permitted to grow longer than usual for the occasion. He had wanted Jo to join them in the receiving line, as the party was also in honour of her birthday, but she had firmly refused.

None of the guests except the Latours were known to her and she wanted to be inconspicuous. Josephine Thornton's twentieth birthday was of no interest to anyone outside her own family, and her father had supported her decision.

He was rigged out in a court dress belonging to Solange's late husband, which fitted fairly well; a dress coat with black breeches and stockings. He and Madame were good friends since he did not fear her acid tongue, and paid her compliments, which were not insincere, as he genuinely admired her, though he did refer to her as 'the old battleaxe' to his daughter.

Jo and her father stood together in front of the bank of flowers, delphiniums, phlox, hydrangeas, all the blooms of late summer, that filled the huge fireplace, watching the arrival of the glittering throng of guests. There were, as was fitting for that countryside, impersonations of Diane de Poitiers, Madame de Montespan, Agnès Sorel and La Pompadour. There were two Louis XIVs, one of them Charles Latour, several members of the Bonaparte family, Napoleon himself and military costumes of great splendour. Some had resorted to earlier times, and there was a Richard Coeur de Lion, in uncomfortable chain mail, an Eleanor of Aquitaine in sweeping robes and a burly man as Henry II.

'Quite a spectacle,' Roger remarked, 'but where do they all come from?'

'I believe the de Savignys have many friends and connections in the countryside,' Jo told him. 'Some of them have come as far as from Paris.' Thérèse had been her informant.

All the guests wore black velvet masks and were announced by their fictitious names, Gaston, in his element in a velvet coat and white wig, pronouncing them with gusto. A footman also in attendance took the wraps from those who had brought them before they greeted their hosts. Some of the ladies went upstairs to the spare bedroom which had been designated as a powder room, with Louise in charge. Others, after shaking hands, and in many cases kissing the hostesses' cheeks, went straight into the *salon*, where drinks were being handed round.

Watching the kaleidoscope of colour and elegance, Jo thought that this was how the château must have looked in its great days, when its owners changed from their hunting clothes to their gorgeous evening apparel. When the Empress Josephine was announced she looked curiously at the masked but easily recognisable figure of Yolande Latour. Her dress was similar to her own, and she also had a diamond necklace around her throat. Had Marcel given it to her? Jo wondered. Her bared neck and shoulders were a little scrawny, but she moved with elegance and grace, wearing her costume with a royal air. She lingered, talking to Marcel, kissed Solange's cheek, and then Thérèse's, who visibly shrank, and then swept into the *salon*.

'Who's that girl?' Roger asked. 'She acts like the Queen of Sheba.'

'We aren't supposed to recognise anyone,' Jo reminded him, 'but between ourselves, that's Marcel's intended.'

'Marcel's what?' Her father looked bewildered.

'You'll hear all about it later on,' Jo said hastily, not wishing to discuss Marcel's engagement until she must.

'Now look here,' Roger said sternly. 'I esteem Marcel de Savigny, I believe him to be a worthy young man, but he *is* French, and I'll not stand for a resurgence of past amours.'

It was Jo's turn to look bewildered, wondering if her father could possibly have some inkling of her own involvement with the master of Savigny, but there was no reason why he should take up the cudgels on Yolande's behalf, who was a stranger to him, and he must know she herself had no claim on him. About to ask him to explain himself, she was forestalled by Charles, who came up to them to ask her to dance, and Roger gave her a pat on the shoulder, saying:

'Run along and enjoy yourself.' And as she hesitated, 'Don't bother about me. I'm going to talk to the old lady. I see she's finished receiving and would probably like some refreshment.'

Charles led Jo into the *salon* where a waltz was in progress. If Marcel had the wrong figure for Napoleon, Charles' shape was even more so for the Sun King, who had been a small man, wearing high heels to give him height. Charles was tall and weedy, but his brocade costume was magnificent.

'You have not come as Madame de Montespan,' he said reproachfully.

'I couldn't manage a hoop, and someone else has had that idea.'

He encircled her with his arm and they began to dance, as he continued:

'You make a better Empress than Yo. She is stately enough, but Josephine was a gracious woman and Yo looks like sour wine.'

'Not very complimentary to your sister, are you?' Jo remarked. 'But what's biting her? I thought she would be on top of the world, and in any case I'm not representing the Empress but a lady of that period, and you're not supposed to know anybody's identity.'

'As if you could disguise yourself from me! I have

missed you while you have been ill, and I hope you are quite recovered?'

'Oh, I'm fine, but I've been in circulation for some time now, and I haven't seen you around the château.'

Charles looked embarrassed. '*Eh bien*, there were reasons, I had to support Yo, *vous savez*?' Jo didn't, but supposed it was something to do with her notoriety over the horse. 'Quite a heroine you have been, *n'est-ce pas*?' he went on. 'I suppose Marcel is lost in admiration.'

'Not so you'd notice,' said Jo, 'to the de Savignys publicity is anathema. To me Lucifer was more important.'

'Such a tender heart! Would you do as much for a mere man?'

'Depends upon the man, but men can usually defend themselves.'

'I am defenceless before your bright eyes,' Charles declared dramatically. 'You should pity me.'

'You can't see my eyes properly,' Jo retorted prosaically.

'They shine through your mask.' And he trod upon her toe.

'Suppose you pay more attention to the dance and less to my eyes,' Jo suggested cruelly, because he had hurt her.

'Ah, *pardon*, I am *maladroit*, but though these masks are no disguise, they are an excuse for a little licence. May I take you into the garden and make love to you?'

'You may not, and Marcel is coming towards us.'

'Unmasked and looking like a thundercloud.' Charles had glanced over his shoulder. They had halted by one of the tall windows. Charles still had his arm about Jo's waist and Marcel was threading his way towards them with displeasure plain in his face. Jo's heart throbbed uneasily as she beheld his splendid dark-clad figure, but she had no idea how she could have annoyed him.

'Excuse me,' said the master of Savigny suavely, though his blue eyes were glacial. 'My grandmother wishes to have a word with you, Charles, before she retires, so if you can tear yourself away from your charming partner, perhaps you would go to her.'

'I am honoured,' Charles returned drily, without removing his arm. 'We have not visited the château for some time and I am surprised she has remembered my existence.'

'She has not been well,' Marcel told him curtly. 'Doubtless she wants to make her apologies.'

'*Eh bien*, a request from her is a command.' Charles reluctantly removed his arm from Jo's waist. 'I regret to leave you, Josephine, but I will soon return, and you will dance with me again?'

'Perhaps,' Jo said provocatively, and Marcel frowned.

'*A bientot, ma mie*,' said Charles as he took himself off.

'What was that he called you?' Marcel demanded as Charles disappeared.

'What you called me when you gave me the diamonds. I'm not sure what it means.'

'He has no right to be so familiar!' Marcel was scowling and Jo wondered if he could possibly be jealous. He was being a dog in the manger if he were.

'As an old family friend he considers himself privileged,' she said sweetly. 'He'd just invited me to go into the garden with him, since a little licence is permitted at masked balls.'

'Would you have gone if I had not intervened?'

'Possibly.'

'I would have wrung your neck if you had,' he said savagely.

'Oh, Marc, such a display of temper, and people are looking at us!'

Curious glances were being thrown by the gyrating couples towards the pair by the window.

Marcel seemed to recollect himself. 'I must go and make sure Charles is not boring Grand'mère. Now, no tricks tonight, if you please, Jo. It is important you appear dignified.'

'I'm afraid that's rather beyond my powers,' Jo returned, wondering how it could possibly matter to him how she conducted herself when his mind must be full of his forthcoming announcement. Perhaps that was it. She was staying at the château and he wanted all its denizens to be on their best behaviour out of respect for his future wife.

'Nothing is beyond your powers when you set your mind to it,' he told her. 'I am only asking you to use them in a right and decorous direction to do credit to us both.'

'Reckon yu be asking a moighty lot of a stable lad, mister,' Jo drawled.

'Oh, you are incorrigible!' Marcel laughed. Then someone called him and he left her abruptly.

Jo watched him disappear with wistful eyes, reflecting that he had not asked her to dance, and now she had alienated him with her mischievous tongue. Well, it was better so. It would have been too bittersweet to be held in his arms knowing it was for the last time.

She did not lack for partners after that, for, emboldened by being masked, a number of young men, and older men too, requested the pleasure. She saw Charles return to the *salon*, but managed to elude him. She was paid heavy compliments in French which she only half understood. She laughed and flirted as if she had not a care in the world, though her heart was heavy with a sense of loss, but she refused all invitations to go into the garden. She passed Marcel dancing with Yolande as she waltzed with Richard Coeur de Lion, and resisted a vulgar desire to put out her tongue at him, as she saw he was frowning at her. The mail-clad arm was holding her too closely for comfort, but she made no protest as it seemed to annoy Marcel. Yolande looked peeved, and Jo wondered vaguely what had displeased her, for as she had told Charles, she should be on top of the world.

Supper time approached, but Jo had no intention of being present in the dining room when Marcel made his announcement. Her father, confident she was enjoying herself, was playing cards in another room. Jo went up to her bedroom, but did not feel safe there; Thérèse or Roger might miss her and come in search of her, and she would feel happier out in the open air. Slipping on a dark coat, she went out into the gallery and choosing a moment when the hall appeared to be deserted, ran down the stairs and escaped through the open front door.

Those couples who had sought the concealing darkness to carry on their amours had gone inside in search of refreshment, and the grounds seemed to be deserted. Jo made for the shrubbery which concealed the stabling. There were seats within its sheltering greenery put there for those who wanted to meditate or flirt in a secluded spot, but now they were empty. Jo sat down on one in the deepest shadow, prepared for a lonely vigil. The party would break up when all the healths had been drunk, the congratulations made, and when she saw the guests dispersing seeking their cars parked behind the château, she would creep back to her room. Meanwhile she tried to concentrate her thoughts upon her welcome home. It would be good to see her mother and sisters again, to ride Bonny into the forest . . . no, not the forest, Marcel's ghost would still linger there, but with the start of harvest she would be too busy to have time to brood.

She was changed, she knew that; the lighthearted girl who had groomed her horses on the morning after Marcel's arrival had gone for ever. He had told her he would teach her to become a woman, and she had learned her lesson well.

CHAPTER ELEVEN

FROM where Jo was sitting the château looked unreal and theatrical, with its façade outlined in coloured lights, and its uncurtained downstairs windows brilliantly lit from within. Marcel had told her she would become used to living in it when upon first seeing it she had been overawed by its size. She had done that up to a point, but she had never felt it was a home; it was more like living in a hotel.

Music and laughter floated out into the night air through open windows and doors, for the hired orchestra was still playing. Jo looked away from the building to the straight avenue of the drive, where more lights were strung from tree to tree as far as the entrance gate, a romantic approach to a fairy-tale edifice, but romance was scorned by its owner, who was contracting a mercenary marriage tonight; all this was the trimming to disguise that sordid fact.

Jo would like to leave on the morrow, and this was her last night but one at Savigny, and it was nearly tomorrow now, but her father had insisted that they would need a day's rest to recover from the festivities, so she must endure the post-engagement congratulations and pretend indifference for another forty-eight hours, disguising the gnawing pain in her heart. It had been a very long day, starting with the bestowal of presents. Because of the uncertainty of foreign mail, she had not heard from her family; they were keeping their greetings and presents for her return. Thérèse had given her scent, Solange an antique brooch, and Marcel the diamonds, which she was determined to return; even though she was sitting in shadow and the starlight was dim, the reflected light from the château caused them to glitter when she moved. She and her father had combined to give Thérèse a crystal dressing table set, which Jo had known she coveted, but the morning with its birthday presents and flurry of final preparations seemed very far away tonight.

Jo sighed and wondered how long it would be before the party broke up and she could seek the sanctuary of her room. She was not wearing a watch, but it must be past midnight. Continentals always kept late hours, and tonight was an occasion. Tomorrow Yolande would be preening herself as the future mistress of Savigny, and plans would be put in hand for the renovation of the château. Quite possibly she would order the smooth lawns to be dug up and install formal flowerbeds, which were a feature of so many châteaux, the plants sternly disciplined in intricate designs. Holding the purse strings, Yolande would be in control and Marcel, no longer master of his own domain, would seek more congenial distractions in Paris, returning now and then to father the children which would be necessary to carry on his name. Such was the pattern of marriages of convenience, Jo thought, but what a travesty of the love and companionship her parents enjoyed in their so satisfactory union.

So lost was she in her depressing thoughts, she did not notice the dark figure approaching her, until it called her name. The faint gleam of the jewels about her neck had betrayed her presence.

'Jo? *C'est toi? Je t'ai cherchée partout.*'

Searching for her? She had recognised Marcel's voice,

but what did he want of her tonight of all nights? He had spoken in French and it flashed into her mind that it was Yolande he was seeking, and the name he had called was Yo. It might be Yolande was acting coyness, causing Marcel to have to find her before he claimed her before the assembled company. She had looked sulky in the *salon*, and they might have had a tiff. A little demon of mischief prompted Jo to play up to his mistake. She had often wanted to imitate Yolande's high shrill voice, and this was her opportunity. She said:

'*Tu me cherches?*' Her French had improved since she had come to the château. '*Ah, Marc, il faisait trop chaud à l'intérieur et je désirais être seule.*'

She held her breath, wondering if she had used the right words. Evidently she had deceived him, for he reached for her hands and drew her to her feet.

'Come, *mignonne*, do not be shy, they are waiting for you in the *salle-à-manger* where I am going to claim you as my betrothed.' Disturbed by his proximity, the close clasp of his hands, Jo did not notice that he was speaking in English, but she resisted as he tried to lead her away, and he went on:

'Perhaps a little preliminary wooing will give you confidence to face the ordeal in front of you.'

Freeing one of her hands, he slid his arm round her shoulders to draw her closer to him, and his voice was half tender, half mocking, not the way he usually spoke to Yolande at all, and Jo stiffened under his arm, thinking what a fraud he was, for she was certain he did not love Yolande, he was marrying her for her dowry. Naturally Yolande would expect some demonstration of affection from him, and he was giving her her money's worth by apeing the ardent lover, but what a farce it all was! His other arm was about her waist, and he bent his head. She knew he was going to kiss her, but she could not accept kisses intended for Yolande. With a sudden movement she wrenched herself free and backed away from him.

'I'm not Yolande Latour,' she told him coldly.

To her astonishment he returned.

'I never supposed you were. Your imitation was very good,' he laughed amusedly, 'but her voice is not quite so shrill, nor her accent so deplorable. They say the French spoken in the Val de Loire is the best in France. Besides, I left Yo in the *salon*.'

'Then why . . .'

He interrupted her sternly;

'Your behaviour tonight, *ma chère*, has been quite outrageous. I am thankful Grand'mère was not there to witness it. Then to cap it all you have to hide yourself in the shrubbery. We could not think what had become of you. What imp has possessed you now?'

'You've no right to scold me,' Jo said indignantly. 'Did Mademoiselle Latour complain that I was disgracing the sedate atmosphere of the château? I noticed she was looking more than usually sour. But what I do is nothing to do with you or her, and for once I was enjoying myself.'

'Were you, Jo?'

She did not notice the irony in his voice, but rushed on recklessly.

'I was having a good time, and if my conduct offended all your stuck-up friends I don't care. At least the menfolk appreciated me!'

'So I saw . . . damn the lot of them!'

'Why so? Because they wanted to dance with me which you didn't. But I'm forgetting, Mademoiselle Latour would not have liked you to partner me, and

now you'll have to do her bidding, except when you
sneak off on a binge to Paris. Thank God I'll soon be
home and can forget this place and all that's happened
here!' She spoke recklessly, easing some of the pain and
jealousy that had made that interminable evening a torment to her. She went on:

'Now, if you'll let me pass, I'll go up to my room
while you get on with your celebrating, and remove my
offending presence from your sight.'

Marcel did not move, but stood in front of her,
blocking her retreat, a dark menacing figure.

'You are talking a lot of nonsense, Josephine,' he told
her in his best Comte de Savigny manner. 'You are
coming in with me to supper.'

'I'll do no such thing!' She tried to slip by him, but he
caught her arm and swung her round to face him. 'Let
me go, Marc,' she pleaded, her control breaking. 'I . . . I
don't want any supper . . . I don't want to see . . .' Her
voice became inaudible.

'Have you forgotten I told you that tonight I would
announce our engagement?'

Forgotten! It had never been far from her mind. That
was why she had fled to the refuge of the shrubbery.

'I haven't had much chance to do that,' she returned
more calmly. 'But I don't think it's an occasion for con-
gratulation.'

'Why ever not?'

'I don't believe in marrying for money.'

'Your father never told me you were an heiress, Jo.'

'Oh, for God's sake, stop baiting me! Ever since
I came here your grandmother has been impressing
upon me how necessary it was for you to marry
Yolande Latour. Tonight you're going to fulfil her
wishes.'

'Oh, *Bon Sang*!' He sounded exasperated, and his fingers dug painfully into her arm. 'Have I not explained there never was and never will be an engagement between her and me? I have always treated that infant betrothal as a joke, but I see Grand'mère has been working upon your credulity, and that is why you are always throwing her up at me. No, Jo, the engagement I am going to announce, and I do not think it will be against your wishes, is yours and mine.'

Jo stood perfectly still, unable to believe her ears. True, on that memorable night he had not mentioned any names and she had taken it for granted that he meant Yolande. He went on:

'Do you imagine I would venture to reprimand you if I had not a personal interest in your behaviour? I was incensed because your conduct tonight was unworthy of the future Madame de Savigny.'

She should have been overwhelmed with delight, but his cold, censorious tone angered her, and she could not rid herself of a feeling that this was some sort of gigantic hoax to humiliate her.

'Is this another charade, Marcel?' she asked.

'*Sacré nom de Dieu!*' his hands gripped her shoulders, shaking her. 'God grant me patience, you little devil! First you drive me mad with jealousy, and now you refuse to take me seriously!'

Then she was in his arms and he was kissing her with increasing savagery, as if he had indeed reached the end of his restraint. Jo went limp against him. This at least was real, the passion that had always lurked below the surface of their dealings together had flared into a consuming flame. He was crushing her hard against him, the jewelled buttons on his waistcoat pressing into her soft flesh; her painstakingly erected coiffure tumbling about her shoulders, while his burning mouth scorched her neck, shoulders, and bruised her mouth. Jo's brain ceased to function, as, oblivious of pain, she surrendered to mindless ecstasy. She would not have resisted if he had tried to take her there and then under the bushes. She was all his and eager to give whatever he required of her.

But Marcel, older than she, was more conscious of time and place, and as he had said before, this was neither. Slowly his constricting embrace slackened, his kisses ceased, as he regained control of himself. Gently he loosed her clinging arms from about his neck, and holding her by her upper arms said jerkily:

'You will . . . have to tidy yourself . . . before you can appear in public.'

Jo realised the disorder of her hair, and dress, the coat fallen about her feet, but those were small matters compared with what had happened.

'So you really mean it,' she said with childish wonder.

'I have always meant it. Don't you know I love you passionately?'

'You didn't act like it when I . . .' she swallowed convulsively, the memory still rankled, '. . . came to your room.'

'But I told you it would not do. I would have shown you very poor respect to take you in that hole-and-corner fashion. But you betrayed that you love me . . . you do, don't you, Jo?'

'Of course I do,' she admitted honestly. 'That's what hurt. I was sure you meant to marry that stupid Yolande.'

He laughed, then said seriously:

'I always meant to marry you, Jo, even when you swiped me across the face in the forest. You have enough of the devil in you to make me a most exciting wife. I came to Greyfriars to buy a horse and obtain a wife. Since I must marry I thought I would like to cement the long friendship between our families and scotch Grand'mère's plans for forcing Yolande on me once and for all. You were my choice, but you were such a wild creature. It was a challenge to woo you, to make you fall for me. You played right into my hands by going to the Pelican. I was sure that once I got you here, the rest would be easy.'

'Relying upon your invincible charm?' Jo asked sarcastically, not appreciating the way she had been manipulated.

'*Eh bien*, whatever it was, it worked.' Marcel released her, and stared away down the drive with its glittering lights. 'What I had not expected was that I should fall deeply and irrevocably in love with you. What it cost me to send you away that night, you will never realise, and then when you were ill, I was nearly distracted, but my presence disturbed you so I had to content myself by providing every care and attention. Did you really think I was a devil, Jo?'

'Of course, after the havoc you'd wrought in my life,' Jo laughed. 'The punishments you'd threatened.' She sobered. 'I wasn't myself, Marcel, and you were all mixed up with fantasies. I didn't recognise you. And after that there was Lucifer.'

'So like you to rush off in his defence regardless of consequences. I think I could have saved him without your help—not that I want to belittle your efforts. Your loyalty made me love you all the more, that and your refusal of the diamonds. I have never known a woman to refuse diamonds before.'

Jo moved restlessly. 'Have you given many women diamonds?' she asked bluntly, not liking the idea.

He turned back to face her and said seriously:

'You said yourself I must have had mistresses, and there have been several affairs, but nothing that went deep. I am a man and a Frenchman, you could not expect me to be a saint.'

'I don't think any the worse of you for that,' Jo told him, pleased by his frankness. 'I prefer a man with experience. But why did you not tell me you weren't going to marry Yolande?'

He laughed wickedly. 'I thought a little jealousy might help you to know your own mind, and I never said I *was* going to marry her. I told you I was going to announce our engagement at the ball, and that is what I am going to do, but first we must make you look respectable or they will think it is ... ahem ... overdue.'

'We can't get into the château without being seen,' Jo pointed out, caring little what she looked like.

'There is a cloakroom in the groom's flat over the stables,' Marcel told her, being a man of resource. 'There will be no one there now, except the Doberman, and he and you are old friends.'

Marcel helped her to do her hair, showing a deftness which surprised her. During the operation, she said to him:

'But Madame de Savigny and Daddy, how are they going to take all this?'

'Grand'mère has accepted the inevitable, your father has been cognisant from the start. That is why he agreed to your visit to France. He did not want to stand in your way, and he prefers me for a son-in-law to Terry Robinson, who seemed to be the alternative.'

'In fact you were a pair of conspirators,' Jo said indignantly. 'You ought to be ashamed of yourselves!'

'We are not in the least, since the end justified the means.' Marcel glanced in the direction of the château. 'There is one thing more—will you be disappointed if we do not live in that great pile?'

'No, it would be a relief. I've not got the makings of a Comtesse de Savigny. Thérèse said something about a farm, that's much more me.'

'It is a quite delightful place, but not nearly so impressive.'

'Marcel, I would be happy in a mud hut so long as you were there.' He moved towards her. 'No, don't embrace me or all this hairdressing will have to be done again. But what about your grandmother? You said you must keep the château for her sake.'

'Unfortunately it does not suit her rheumatism. She has agreed to rent a villa at Roscoff, where she can get special treatment. I think we must allow Thérèse to go to Paris. She has an idea she would like to study music, so it will be just you and I together, *ma chérie*.'

'What could be better?' Jo said happily as they left the flat. She glanced towards Lucifer's box. 'And Luci will be coming too?'

'Yes, he will be going to the farm. He began it all.'

'I reckon yu be roight, bor,' and she touched an imaginary cap.

But there was no vestige of the hoyden Jo as she entered the glittering dining room on Marcel's arm, an elegant lady clad in silk and diamonds, to be acclaimed Marcel's bride-to-be. As the toasts were drunk and the babble of congratulations broke out around them, she whispered to him:

'Have I acquired those social graces, Marc?'

'*Chérie*, you are marvellous,' he assured her.

'But I'm still the same old Jo underneath.'

Marcel grinned.

'I would not have you otherwise, *mon garçon*.'

Experience the warmth of . . .

Harlequin Romance

The original romance novels.
Best-sellers for more than 30 years.

Delightful and intriguing love stories
by the world's foremost writers
of romance fiction.

Be whisked away to dazzling
international capitals . . .
or quaint European villages.
Experience the joys of falling in love . . .
for the first time, the best time!

Harlequin Romance

A uniquely absorbing journey
into a world of superb romance reading.

**No one touches the heart of a woman
quite like Harlequin!**